HEART BEAT
By Lynne Waite Chapman

Published by Take Me Away Books, a division of Winged Publications

Copyright © 2017 by Lynne Waite Chapman

ISBN-13: 978-1-946939-25-8
ISBN-10: 1-946939-25-0

Chapter One

I hustled from my car to The Rare Curl, thinking I'd kill for another cup of coffee. My teeth were chattering. Goosebumps up my arms—in May. My sweater wasn't doing the job. Should've grabbed a jacket, maybe gloves. My coworkers, Rarity and Stacy, would have had a good laugh if I'd shown up with gloves. They told me living in Florida had given me thin blood, if there was such a thing. Back in Evelynton a year, and still not accustomed to the northern Indiana climate.

I reached for the salon door just in time for it to slam against my knuckles. Ouch. I rubbed my hand against my sweater. A bruised hand is small sacrifice to keep from getting smacked in the face by the heavy door.

Patricia Martin, local dress shop owner, stomped out. Our eyes met for a moment through the glass. Without a word, she went on her way.

So, I guess no apology.

And I'd thought she was finally beginning to like

me. She'd been one of those who labeled me the poor widowed Lauren Grace James, come home for the sake of the pitiful inheritance of an old house and an old car. The woman who'd failed at life, with no place to go. Perceptions were slow to change in a small town, but people were getting to know me. Most had upgraded my identity to Lauren Halloren, magazine writer and part-time receptionist.

Patricia stood at her Mercedes and fumbled with her key fob until the lock popped. She climbed in, revved the engine, and backed into the roadway without looking. Oncoming traffic obliged her by making space.

Some people led charmed lives.

Shaking my sore hand, I reached once more for the door handle. The reception room and service area appeared empty, but I caught a glimpse of Rarity, my boss, as she disappeared into the supply room.

Wonder what was with Patricia? It wasn't like Rarity to anger a customer, or anyone, ever. Maybe Patricia expected a last-minute appointment and Rarity couldn't accommodate her. Still, irate customers were rare at The Rare Curl. I grinned at my little word play.

After stashing my handbag in the bottom drawer of my desk, I scanned the appointment book. Patricia did have an appointment, first on the list. She should've been sitting in Rarity's styling chair, coffee in hand, not motoring through town, endangering Evelynton citizens.

The rusty hinge on the supply room door squawked, followed by the tap of Rarity's sensible heels closing in behind me. In the year since she hired me, I've learned to recognize her gait The woman had a way of crossing the room, not really at a run, but hard to describe as a walk.

"I've lost my mind. Don't know what's happened. It's all gone." Rarity sputtered over my shoulder.

"What?" I swiveled my chair to peer into her eyes. "You're not joking."

The attractive laugh lines that bracketed her green eyes had morphed into stress creases. Perspiration dotted her forehead. Heat radiated from her body.

"What's going on? Are you okay? Is Stacy alright?"

"I'm fine. Um, we're fine. It's the supplies. My hair color is gone." Rarity pulled in a deep breath and blew it out between her lips. "Did you see Patricia leave?"

"I sure did. Almost lost my hand in the process." I massaged my throbbing knuckles.

"She was so upset. Poor thing was supposed to get her hair tinted this morning. She drove all the way in here, and I had to tell her I couldn't do it."

Poor thing? Patricia? I bet she'd never been disappointed before. Wouldn't hurt to hear no for once. "I'm sure she'll be fine. She'll understand it was an accident."

Rarity pulled a tissue from her pocket and dabbed at the corners of her eyes. "We'll have to call her, but wait a while, 'til she cools off. Oh dear, would you call Rhonda, my next appointment, and tell her I can't color her hair today? I hope she isn't already on her way."

"Absolutely. Right away. When should I rebook

3

her appointment?"

"First available, tomorrow. Er… call all my color appointments. Work them in over the next few days, wherever you find a spot. I'll start early and stay late, whatever works."

"Don't worry. Your ladies aren't about to get mad at you for one little problem. I've never seen you mess up in all the time I've worked here."

Rarity worried the tissue into shreds. "Oh Lauren, it's the second time this week. I don't know what's going on. There were only a couple of bottles on the shelves this morning. And I just restocked on Saturday. At least I think I did." She placed a palm on her forehead for a moment before continuing.

"That morning—Saturday—we were short on supplies, we shouldn't have been, but I ran to the supply house to restock. Funny thing is, I was sure I brought back plenty to last us. I didn't think I needed to check the inventory again last night. I should have. I went in to mix Patricia's formula, and we're out. It was all gone."

"Don't worry. There's a good explanation. You must have been busier than you realized yesterday. And that's a good thing, isn't it?" This conversation was stretching my abilities. I'm not usually the one who had to encourage my older and wiser employer.

"I don't know. Didn't think so, but…" She stuffed the scraps of tissue into her pocket.

"All this extra work is asking a lot. As soon as I'm sure things are under control here, I'll drive to the supply house."

I picked up the handset and dialed. "I'm on it, Rarity. Oh, what about Stacy? Is she okay with her customers?"

"I have her checking her appointments against the stock right now. Move all my haircut and shampoo-set appointments together for later today. It'll take me a couple hours to get to the city and back. This time I'll be sure to pick up enough to cover us until the regular shipment comes in."

The red splotches in her cheeks began to fade to her natural peach blush, although her voice still held a noticeable tremor.

"Hello Rhonda. It's Lauren at The Rare Curl."

I glanced up to see Rarity standing with her hands covering her face. "Sorry Rhonda, hold on a minute."

I put my hand over the mouthpiece of the phone and tried to speak to Rarity in a soft, reassuring voice. "It's going to be okay. As soon as I talk to Rhonda, I'll get everyone else moved."

She pulled her hands away. "Yes, I know it will be okay."

Rarity raised her eyes to the ceiling and counted on her fingers. "An hour to get there, half hour at the store, an hour back. Book my appointments beginning at one o'clock—no two. I can get them done and still go to Bible study tonight." She took a deep breath and grinned.

The supply room door squawked open and slammed against the wall. "Lauren!" Stacy approached at a run. "Give me the phone. I gotta call my first two women. There's no hair color for them." She froze, eyes glazed and mouth open. "Wait, do we have any perms? Mrs. Brubaker is coming in for a permanent wave this afternoon." She spun on her heel and loped back to the supply room.

Rarity stared after Stacy, and I rushed to explain the situation to Rhonda, still waiting on the line.

A minute later, the door to the backroom banged against the wall again.

Out of breath from the trek to and from the supply room, Stacy puffed. "Nope, no perms. I'll have to call everybody."

She glared at her employer. "Rarity, what happened? We're completely out of stock. How could you let us get this low? Seriously, I don't know where your mind's been this month."

Rarity shook her head. "I'm so sorry, Stacy. Can't imagine what happened. I was sure we had enough to last us. Call your ladies. Tell them it's my fault and I'll have everything fixed by tomorrow. I'll even give them a discount for the inconvenience. I'm driving to the supply house right away." She pulled her handbag over her shoulder and waved on her way out.

Still trying to explain the situation to Rhonda, I felt white heat from Stacy's eyes burrowing into my back—right between the shoulder blades. The incessant tapping of her foot distracted me so much I could barely hear the woman on the phone.

I spun around to face Stacy, gave a shrug, and held the receiver tighter, lest she grab it away.

She pivoted and stomped to her styling station, muttering all the way. Something about the discount likely coming out of her pay.

Reaching her styling station, she plopped into her chair and shouted across the room. "I'll use my cell phone. Rarity refuses to hire anyone new. I'm already doing double duty with all Patsy's customers, and now this. What a screw-up."

I cupped my hand around the mouthpiece. "I'm so sorry. I don't know what that ruckus is. Something from the street."

Two hours later, I'd finished my calls and pried the phone from my ear. No conversation with the women of Evelynton was ever short, but there were no complaints. Even Patricia had gotten over the indignity of it all, and calmed by the time I spoke to her.

Stacy finished her calls though their reaction was a mystery. Customers tend to mirror the attitude of the stylist, and that wasn't such a good thing today.

But tragedy averted, serenity returned to The Rare Curl. The remainder of my four-hour shift proceeded peacefully.

~

Rarity, experienced hairdresser and business owner, had always been rock steady. I guess that's why the Tuesday morning chaos fled my mind as soon as I returned home to the cozy Cape Cod I'd inherited from my Aunt Ruth.

Stepping over the threshold, I barely had time to deposit my bag before Mason flew into my arms. What would I do without his welcome—his warm body next to mine? I'd thought myself a loner, but there had been no resisting once this guy had decided to move in with me.

Mason snuggled close and nuzzled my chin. I giggled as he rubbed his fuzzy face across my cheek.

Mason's my cat, the golden-eyed, black and white feline who'd adopted me almost as soon as I arrived in Evelynton.

"Enough, Mason. Get down and I'll check your

food bowl. You'll have to leave me alone this afternoon and tomorrow. I have to finish that magazine article on time. We'll need the income if we're both going to eat this month."

Mason pounced to the floor and tailed me to the kitchen where I filled his bowl. I left him to choose bits of kibble. While I changed clothes, thoughts ran through my mind of the day's events. Was someone stealing from The Rare Curl? Or was Rarity losing her mind?

Chapter Two

Thursday morning, on my way to work, I realized the salon was far from my mind last night, but as I approached the front door, I recalled my bruised knuckles, and peeked through the glass to make sure I wouldn't collide with an irate customer.

The waiting room sat vacant. Stacy's first customer was in her styling chair. The two laughed as snips of hair flew.

Everything back to normal.

I'd stored my handbag in my desk when the supply room door screeched with Rarity's standing in the door.

"Lauren, come back and look at this, please." I heard it in her voice. The same twinge of stress I'd witnessed Tuesday.

I went straight to the supply room. Rarity's eyes and mouth sagged like I'd never seen before. "I restocked those shelves Tuesday afternoon. You remember, I was going to the supply house? Now look. More than half of the products are missing. We used some yesterday, of course, but there should have been lots left over."

Rarity turned to the shelves and picked through the bottles. "Two, no three auburn, and two of the dark brown. Thank goodness, I think there's enough to get by today—barely."

"Really? I guess I've never paid attention to this room, so I don't know how many bottles are usually here."

Rarity ran her hands through her hair, causing red curls to stand up and away from her face. "There should be lots. I don't know what's going on. Must be losing my mind."

"You are not losing your mind." At least I hoped not. Rarity was a good fifteen to twenty years older than me. At what age does dementia usually show up?

"Think back. If you bought extra, maybe you stored some."

"No. I'm sure I didn't. There's plenty of room on these shelves." Her eyes darted round the room. "I don't know where I would have put them. There isn't any other space."

Even as she spoke, Rarity pulled out bins from under the counter and searched the contents.

I poked my head under the sink, finding two cans of scouring powder, a large bottle of glass cleaner, and three rolls of paper towels. After that, I wandered into the bathroom. Weird place to look, I know. But there have been times I've discovered my cell phone in the refrigerator.

I returned to the supply room and stood in the doorway. "Nothing there. You?"

Rarity leaned against the sink. Her voice came in a hoarse whisper. "No. Nothing."

"Do you think someone is pilfering your supplies?"

"No. I can't believe it. But that's the only explanation, isn't it? Unless it's Alzheimer's." Rarity pressed her fingers to her temple. "I think my Uncle Nathan had that."

"Rarity, you don't have Alzheimer's. You've just been busy lately. Probably too much to keep track of. Did you bring all the bottles in? Maybe you left them in the car."

"Oh. I might have." Rarity brightened, and in typical fleet-footed fashion, grabbed her keys and streaked outside, only to plod back in a few minutes later.

"I was hoping to find a bag in the trunk. Better to have forgotten to bring them in than to lose them. Nothing."

I searched my brain for an explanation. "The only answer is someone got in here and stole from you."

Lines spread across Rarity's forehead. "Oh no. That can't be it."

She stopped and raised her eyes to mine. "But why? What would anyone want with so many bottles of hair color?" We both whirled around to peer into the salon where Stacy fluffed her customer's hair.

Rarity turned to me and shook her head. "No, not Stacy. She's worked for me for years. I have complete faith in her."

I agreed with a head shake of my own. "No. It wouldn't be Stacy. But those supplies went someplace. Who else has had access?"

"Nobody." She sucked in a deep breath and continued. "I can't imagine. This has never happened before."

"Let's think it through." I held up one finger. "The first time you noticed missing supplies was on Saturday. Is that correct?"

"Yes, Saturday morning, so I went and bought more."

I ticked another finger. "Then, when I came in on Tuesday, you didn't have any hair color."

She nodded. "That's right, so I purchased replacements."

Third finger up. "And today is Thursday, more missing. This is crazy." Remembering Rarity's doubts of her own sanity, I regretted the word choice.

"Yes. It seems as though someone steals my supplies, waits for me to replenish the shelves, and then comes in the next day to take more. You're right, it is crazy. Or I am. You don't think I'm imagining all this, do you?"

I didn't have time to answer. Rarity raised her hands. "I bet I left them at the store. I'll call the supply house and ask if I left a bag on the counter." She raised her eyes to the ceiling. "Maybe I should ask if I was even there."

Couldn't come up with any more reassuring words, so I followed her to the reception desk where she made the call.

When Rarity hung up the phone, she put her hands on her hips and smiled. "I was there Saturday, and again on Tuesday."

"I knew they would confirm it. And did they find your supplies?"

"No. I didn't leave any on the counter. But it's good to know I'm not imagining things."

I lowered my voice and leaned closer to Rarity. "Shoot. We're back to theft. They must sneak in at night. This is a small place. You'd notice someone wandering into the storeroom during the day. They picked the lock, or they have a key. Who has keys?"

"I do, of course. And Stacy." She threw her hands in the air. "That's all. You don't even have one, do you? And I retrieved Patsy's key when she was arrested."

"Unless she had it copied for some reason. But she's in prison and who would have access to her stuff? Her husband's dead, and so's her boyfriend."

I pulled a pad of paper from the desk drawer and listed the days the supposed thefts occurred. "So if they keep to that schedule, they will be back on Friday night. Or they might not. Maybe tonight. I'm confused. But you can't keep buying supplies, only to have them disappear. Rarity, you'd better call the police."

Rarity's eyes snapped to me. "Oh no. It can't be that serious. I've been thinking. It's probably kids. You know how all the teenagers, boys as well as girls, are playing with hair color now."

I didn't know that. There were no teenagers in my life.

Rarity continued. "And look, nothing else is missing Of everything of value here in the salon, only hair color has disappeared and a couple perms.

"That's it." Rarity laughed. "What a relief. It's kids, and they're only having fun with it. If I involved the law, a child's life would be ruined." She slowly shook her head. "I couldn't bear it."

"What are we going to do?"

She raised an index finger. "Before I even think of speaking to the police, we'll discover who it is and talk to them. I'll explain the consequences of their actions. I think that's the best plan. Don't you?"

No, I didn't.

But Rarity's eyes sparkled again and her sweet smile returned.

I let out a sigh. "Maybe. I guess serious criminals would take more. You're right, it's probably kids."

She laid a finger on the side of her head. "How do I figure out who it is? Wallace would know what to do, but he's out of town for a week."

"He's a gem, Rarity. You should marry him. You're right. He would know what to do. I always feel secure with him living right next door to me. Sort of think of him as the neighborhood guard. But he's not here, so let me consider this. I'll come up with a plan."

Hold on. Did I say I'd come up with a plan? Who was I kidding? I'd begun to believe the inflated stories of my crime-fighting skills.

It all stemmed from an incident a year ago. I guess I'd forgotten it was my neighbor, Wallace, who'd been the true hero, tackling Patsy as she ran from my house. He'd slipped away without even getting his name on the police report, leaving me in the limelight.

Rarity's eyes brightened. "Would you, Lauren? You are so good at these things." She knew better. I'm sure her gentleman friend, Wallace, told her all about it.

Rarity patted her curls back into place and straightened her blouse. "Right now, it's business as usual. We give the best service possible to our clients."

She flashed me a big smile. "I'll be waiting to hear your plan."

Chapter Three

T hanks Lauren. I don't need a bag." Mrs. Phillips carried her new bottle of shampoo to the door. The bells, attached to the handle, jingled as the door opened, and again as it closed. A few seconds later they rang as one of Stacy's friends stepped in to say hello.

The Rare Curl was a busy place. People were in and out all day, for hairstyles, hair spray, or most of all, gossip. That's the way it went for the next hour of my shift. Those bells signaled each movement of the front door, but I tried to keep my mind on my work.

I'd begun to fantasize about how far I could throw the bells, when Murine Baron sauntered into the salon.

I'd known her for a year. The woman never sauntered. A scurry, at best. Today, there was a spring in her step.

The Barons were my neighbors on Stonybridge— opposite side from Wallace. Murine rarely stepped outside. And I exerted a conscious effort to avoid any contact with her husband, Clive. These weren't the neighbors I'd ask about borrowing a cup of sugar.

Murine probably wouldn't answer the door. She reminded me of a mouse—sort of timid and wary.

Clive, on the other hand, wasn't a bit timid. If he looked my way, I felt like the mouse and ran for cover whenever possible. Big, burly, and caveman-ish. A permanent scowl graced his face. And when he walked, I imagined him making dents in the concrete sidewalk.

A regular monthly haircut customer of The Rare Curl, Murine spoke only to her hairdresser, Stacy.

"Good morning, Murine. You look nice today. New sweater? Great shade of pink."

She smiled. "Thank you so much, Lauren. I love it, too."

My mouth fell open. Who was this woman?

"Stacy is expecting you, Murine. Shall I get you a cup of coffee?"

The woman was still smiling. "No, thank you. I got out early and stopped by Ava's Java this morning."

Huh? Murine at one of the busiest gathering spots in town? I was unnerved when she looked me straight in the eyes. Had she ever met my eyes before?

Murine continued to Stacy's styling chair and left me to wonder about the personality change.

Two hours later, she reached across the desk to hand me cash. Not the usual check signed by Clive. One glance at her and I almost dropped the money. Pretty sure my mouth fell open. Her hair had always been dull, dusty brown—sort of mouse color. Now it glistened with golden strands. "Wow. Your hair is beautiful. That's a great new color."

Murine beamed. "Thank you." She turned to leave, and her hair fanned out in the breeze.

As the door swung closed behind Murine, I

swiveled my chair to face Stacy. She swept bits of hair from around her styling station. "What's happened to Murine? I've never seen such a transformation. Hard to believe it's the same woman."

Stacy swished hair into the dustpan. "I know, right? Thought she'd be buried with that frumpy hair. I don't get it. She's hardly ever talked to me since I started cutting her hair. You know, after Patsy went to jail for killing that jerk husband of hers. Anyway, every month, all Murine said was, 'A bit shorter.'" Stacy rolled her eyes. "It was agonizing."

Leaving the dustpan on the floor, Stacy stood, hands planted on her hips.

"Did you see it? Would you believe she let me layer her cut and add color? Boy, was I frantic. Finally got the chance to do something with her hair, and no supplies. We had some bleach, so I talked her into the highlights." Stacy flipped her hair out of her eyes, looking very pleased with herself.

"I wonder what got into her."

"And get this, you must have noticed Murine's clothes. She always wore the same thing. Gray. Always gray. Today, she walked in wearing a new sweater, and wanted a new hairstyle. Miracles still happen." Stacy shook her head, picked up the dustpan and emptied it into the trash container. "Whatever has happened, it's great to see her happy."

"Absolutely. It's just weird."

I turned back to my desk and glanced at the clock. "It's lunch time. I'm taking off. Rarity should be back pretty soon."

"Don't worry about me. I'm hoping to get a walk-in haircut customer to make up for the appointments I had to cancel." Stacy popped a stick of gum into her mouth and waited for me to vacate my place at the reception desk so she could sit in it.

I pushed the door partway open, but caught it in time to avoid it colliding with a motorized wheelchair. The woman riding it sped past without a second look. She must have had it at full throttle. Anything traveling at that speed should be on the street instead of the sidewalk. I don't care if it is technically a wheelchair.

After a second look in both directions, I pushed the door all the way open and shot a wave at Stacy. "See you next week."

With renewed energy, I walked the two blocks to my car.

I hopped in the Chrysler and drove straight home, anxious to get to work. My real work. Writing. It didn't pay much, but I had hopes. After pulling into the drive, I threw the gearshift into park, but hesitated to get out. Someone was in the Baron's backyard.

Branches swung open and Murine pushed through the bushes, a bouquet of bright, deep-purple lilacs dangling from her hand.

I kept my seat, wondering who might be with her. Counted to ten before climbing out of the car.

Yes, I admit it. Clive scared me. My first introduction to the man had been through the blast of his twelve-gauge, when he'd interrupted a prowler in his house. Fortunately, he'd missed and left no dead bodies.

This time Clive didn't appear. The little woman was alone, so I stepped out and waved. "Beautiful flowers, Murine."

"They are, aren't they? I can't wait to put them in a

vase in the living room." She continued up her front steps and into the house.

I gazed up at the maple tree and took a few minutes to listen to sweet bird songs before going inside. Something strange was happening in Evelynton. My confident employer, Rarity, was doubting her sanity. Murine walked with a confident swagger?

Something in the water? Drugs?

Chapter Four

Sometimes I wanted to spend the day at Ava's Java, inhaling the aroma of freshly-ground coffee, snuggled into an overstuffed chair, reading a good book. That coffee aroma and the soothing wall tones of coffee brown and sweet cream softened a mood better than Prozac.

I've never taken Prozac, but I imagined the popular coffee shop was better.

When I walked in, I felt like kicking off my shoes and curling up in one of the comfy chairs. I guessed that would be going a bit too far, even for a regular like me.

While my inherited house had begun to feel homier in the past year, at Ava's, I could always find friendly faces. I'd even begun to call many of them by name. No easy feat for an introverted writer like me.

I'd grown up in Evelynton, but never looked back after I left for college twenty-six years ago. When I was forced to return last year, it wasn't a happy homecoming. Having resisted until there'd been no other choice, my return was a last resort.

So Ava's Java did a lot to endear this small Indiana

town to me. Ava's and my friends, Clair and Anita, who could often be found at our favorite table in the front window.

I walked up to the counter, expecting to greet Ava, but someone new stood behind the counter. Another change? The young girl at the cash register had big brown eyes and a sweet smile.

"Hi. What can I do for you today?"

"I think I'll just have coffee. Light roast with low fat milk in a mug. I'm staying.

The girl pulled a mug from the rack and pivoted toward the coffee maker.

I pushed forward in my quest to get to know people. "Um, you're new here, aren't you?"

"Sort of. I'm Melody. I've been working in the back for a couple of weeks, grinding coffee and organizing things. This morning, Ava said I'm ready for the counter, and here I am."

"Nice to meet you, Melody. I stop in a few times a week, so I'm sure I'll be seeing you again."

As expected, Anita sat at our usual table. I carried my coffee over and slid into the chair across from her. "How's the soup today?"

Anita hummed a positive reply through a mouth full of broth.

I gave her a minute to swallow. "Where's Clair? Working?"

Anita shook her head and dabbed her mouth with a napkin. "She had a lunch date with some new guy, not sure where. I guess she wanted privacy. You know, she's probably afraid we'd be watching his every move and judging his character. And, well, we would."

"Absolutely. She really shouldn't hide from us. We

21

could tell her right away whether he was worth her time. How's she doing on the dating site?"

"Not great. Different guy every couple of days, but nobody special. A bunch of first dates. Ugh. Can you imagine the conversations? 'Have you ever been married?' 'What do you like to do for fun?' 'What's your favorite food?' 'What's your sign?' Over and over, and over again. Wears me out just thinking about it."

"Hadn't thought of it in that light. Sounds stressful."

"No kidding. So, how was work this morning?" Anita dipped her spoon back into the soup.

"Crazy. Rarity's a wreck. Somehow, somebody got in and stole a bunch of hair color and permanent wave lotion. She and Stacy barely had anything to work with. And it's happened before. The first time, or at least the first time Rarity noticed, was last weekend. She had to drive to the supply house to buy more. Then those products disappeared within a day. We figured it's been every other day, as though they wait for her to replace what they stole and come back. I've spent my time calling women, trying to convince them they'd really be happy waiting another week to get their hair done. What a mess."

Anita pushed her bowl aside. "Poor Rarity. She's so kind. Not an enemy in town. I can't imagine who would steal from her. She surely can't afford for that to go on. What do the authorities say?"

I shrugged. "We haven't notified the police."

"What? Why not?"

"Rarity has decided it was probably young people, so she's protective. And you know Rarity, she'd rather take care of it herself."

"Oh yes, I can see her point. She works with the youth group at church. They love her. She's just like one of the kids. I bet if she found out who was doing this, she could make them understand the gravity of the situation."

"Hmm. Maybe." I took a minute to think about the logic. "I guess the first thing we have to do is discover who's involved. Whoever the culprits are, they seem to have a pattern. I'm thinking of watching the salon for a few nights to see who shows up."

"Watch the salon?" Anita's eyes lit up. A smile began to tug at the corners of her mouth. "What, like a stakeout?"

I nodded. "What do you think?"

"Yes! You could hide in the salon and catch them in the act."

"No, I don't think so. Not quite that brave. Besides, where would I hide? There's only the supply room, and that's where the thieves would be going. And there's the bathroom. Either place, I'd be trapped. What if it isn't kids, but some thug?"

Anita stared at me. A furrow forming between her brows. "You're right. We'll have to watch from outside. We could park across the street in the lot."

"Excuse me. Did you say *we*? You're planning on helping?"

"I am absolutely coming along. I'm not going to miss out on this. You had all the fun last year when you captured Patsy."

"I didn't capture... never mind. What will Jake say?"

She flapped a hand at me. "He won't mind. He

never worries about me. It's Evelynton, for goodness sake. Besides, if you see the thieves, you know you won't recognize them, but I will. I know most of the kids in town, as well as their parents. I can help you identify the culprit."

"You're right about that. I could use someone who actually knows people."

Anita's excitement got the better of her and she shouted. "What fun!" She glanced around and ducked her head, whispering, "We're going on a stake out! Will you bring your gun?"

I shook my head. "No. Absolutely not. I promised myself last year to keep that stored away. I hate guns."

Anita sighed. "Okay. This is still so exciting."

I leaned back in my chair while Anita stirred her soup. She made it sound like a trip to the zoo. At least I'd have company.

~

At home, with more time to think through the planned adventure, I paced—first to the kitchen, then to the front door, and back to the kitchen.

Mason fell in step behind me and stayed at my heels for a turn or two, until I picked him up. "What will I do if I see someone breaking in? Even worse, what if I don't see anyone? That'll make for a long night."

Mason purred.

"Should I go back a second night? A third? What if a policeman shows up and asks what we're doing out in the middle of the night?"

I stopped and held Mason up to look him in the eye. "Who came up with this silly scheme?"

Mason meowed at me.

"Yes, I know it was my idea, so hush."

I tucked him under my arm and resumed the trek through the house. "I can't believe I have to sit in a car all night just because Rarity doesn't want to call the police. What if the perps don't stick to the pattern? I don't know if there even is a pattern."

Mason's feet thrashed against me, drawing my attention to his uncomfortable state. "Yowl."

Living alone can make a person a little weird. I put him down. "Sorry, Mason."

Sinking onto the sofa, I leaned over to look into the cat's eyes once again. "Maybe they don't need any more hair products and will stop. I guess that would be a good thing, wouldn't it?"

"Meow."

"Right. What if they escalate? Come back for the computer, or I don't know, maybe the blow dryers?"

Mason turned his tail to me and left the room.

Chapter Five

At eight-fifteen on the dot, tires crunched the gravel in my drive. I checked to see Anita's mini-van parked next to my Chrysler.

I was ready. Black slacks, black sweater, hair in a ponytail. On opening the door, I noticed Anita wore black sweatpants, black sweatshirt, and a navy-blue scarf covering her blond hair.

"Gosh, we look like burglars. Sure hope nobody's looking out their window. In this neighborhood, they'd call the police, for sure."

Anita's eyes got big. She scanned the houses on each side and across the street. "We'd better move fast." She went down the steps, trotted to the Chrysler, and opened the passenger door.

I'd climbed in the driver's side and inserted the key into the ignition when Anita popped out and ran back to her car.

"Be right back."

A moment later, she'd returned carrying a canvas bag. I peeked inside to find a thermos, two cups, and a box of chocolate chip cookies. Anita grinned, her eyes sparkling. "Almost forgot our provisions. Oh, and I brought a flashlight, too."

Maybe the stakeout wouldn't be so bad after all.

The sun had already dipped below the horizon when we drove into the parking lot across from The Rare Curl. I pulled up next to two small trees and killed the engine. We unbuckled our seat belts. I slumped into the seat and made myself comfortable. Anita faced me, leaning against the door with her knees pulled up.

It was cozy for the first two hours. We, mostly Anita, talked nonstop. Then the cookies and the coffee ran out. After my friend rested her head against the seat back, a soft snore was the only sound in the car. Minutes slipped by. I made mental notes for future magazine articles, wrote a grocery list by the light of my cell phone, and wondered if Mason missed me.

After that, I turned to listing reasons a stakeout was a stupid idea. How long should I sit here? All night? If the thief showed up, would I apprehend him? No gun.

I stretched to peer into the backseat. Nothing to use as a weapon. Not even a tire iron, whatever that was.

Who did I think I was, Jessica Fletcher? This was a waste of time.

I twisted toward the steering column and pushed the key all the way into the ignition. Before turning the key, I cast one last glance toward the salon. And I saw a shadow. A dark blob hovered at the side of the building. I hadn't noticed it earlier. The streetlights gave off minimal light, and my eyes were blurry with fatigue. I blinked twice. Maybe it was nothing. No, it stirred.

I blinked again and refocused. The shadow definitely moved. A figure edged from the side of the building and approached the door of the salon. The man, I think it was a man, stood in front of the entrance, and opened the door. He proceeded inside, the door shutting behind him.

I tapped Anita's knee and whispered, "There's someone in the salon."

"Huh? What's going on?" She pulled herself up straight and squinted through the windshield.

A beam of light became visible inside The Rare Curl. We leaned forward, eyes straining to see.

What should we do now? I really hadn't thought this through.

Anita's whisper came in the dark. "Did you see who it was?"

I whispered in return. "No. Just a figure moving to the door. And he couldn't have had time to pick the lock. Must have had a key 'cause he went right in."

Anita raised her voice to a normal level. "You know they can't hear us out here, right?"

"Oh. Yeah."

We sat and stared and waited. After about five minutes, a car rolled to a stop in front of the salon. Its headlights were off. The door of the salon opened, and the interior light of the car came on as the first figure loaded something into the back seat. His head appeared over the top of the car, and he looked in our direction.

Anita slid to the floor of the car and I flopped sideways to lay on the seat.

My friend reached up and grabbed my arm. "Oh no. He saw us. Do you think he can see us in the car?"

I lifted my head enough to peek over the dash. "No, he can't. We're too far away. There aren't any street lights close enough to illuminate the inside of the car."

Crap. Deep in the recesses of my mind, it occurred to me that I drive a thirty-five-year-old Chrysler Station Wagon. How many of those would there be in Evelynton, Indiana? Or any place?

The interior light of the thief's car went out as he shut the rear door and flashed back on briefly as he climbed into the front seat.

I pulled myself upright behind the wheel and poked Anita. "It's okay. Get back on the seat."

The mysterious car crept down the street, the headlights coming on a block away.

I turned the Chrysler's ignition, put it in gear, and pressed the gas pedal, carefully guiding it around the concrete parking barriers. I drove as fast as I could without headlights. I mean, I drove really slow, so I wouldn't crash into anything until we got to the street.

Anita planted her elbows on the dashboard and peered through the windshield, while I strained my eyes and white-knuckled the steering wheel.

We cruised, searching for taillights, car-sized shadows, anything that might become visible while passing under streetlights.

"Can you see anything?"

Anita shook her head. "Nothing. Where did they go?"

"Maybe they're hiding. We can't be that far behind them. Look down the side streets as we pass." We edged along Main Street, finding nothing but empty pavement and alleys.

Anita pushed herself back in her seat. "Darn. We lost them. That didn't work out."

"At least I can tell Rarity she isn't crazy. She can stop doubting herself. There is definitely someone stealing from her, and it isn't her responsibility to save them. I don't think it's kids. The guy looked kind of stocky and there was something about the way he moved. It just felt like a grown man, don't you think?"

Anita shrugged. "I didn't see him."

I pulled the Chrysler into a vacant lot, made a three-point turn, and drove back to The Rare Curl, pulling up close to the curb. Anita retrieved a flashlight from her near-empty goody bag, and we both jumped out of the car.

She flashed the light on the door handle. "No sign of tampering. He must have had a key. Don't touch anything. We don't want to mess up the evidence."

Anita's been watching cop shows.

She pulled her sleeve over her hand and tried to open the door. "Locked."

"Shine the light through the front window."

She placed the flashlight flat against the window, illuminating circular areas inside as she moved it around.

"I don't see anything out of place in there, do you?"

"No, I can't say I see much of anything. This beam of light doesn't go far."

Standing there with faces pressed to the glass, I began to feel conspicuous.

"Let's get out of here before someone sees us, and we have to explain why we're dressed like cat burglars."

We scurried back into the car, and I steered it toward home.

As soon as I dropped Anita at her van and locked myself in the house, I called Rarity to report our findings. And to suggest, again, she notify the authorities.

"Okay, Lauren. You're sure it wasn't teenagers?"

"It didn't seem like kids to me. In any case, this is getting serious. You're losing a lot of money. You can't let it go on."

"I know you're right. I've already had to get into my savings. If you really think it was an adult, I'll call first thing in the morning—after I pray about it. I'll go in tomorrow to see if they took anything, and then I'll call."

Sweet Rarity, always giving everyone the benefit of the doubt.

I clamped my mouth shut to keep from screaming, "Of course they took something! Why do you think they were in there in the middle of the night? Call now!"

I took a deep breath and blew out a sigh. "Okay. I'll meet you at the salon first thing in the morning."

Chapter Six

After a final toss of the covers, I opened my eyes wide enough to peek at the alarm clock. Ugh, fifteen minutes before it was due to go off. I threw off the sheet and stared at the ceiling.

Knowing Rarity, she'd had sweet dreams and a great night's sleep. I, on the other hand, spent the night chasing dark-clad figures in and out of various rooms at The Rare Curl. On one occasion, a man with bright orange hair chased me into the bathroom. I was trapped until Officer Farlow opened the door and shouted "Lauren Halloren, you're under arrest."

How did Farlow get into my nightmare? He wasn't my favorite person in Evelynton, and to be fair, I wasn't his either. I'd had a couple run-ins with him. Once he'd accused me of insurance fraud, or insinuated it, and later suspected me of murder. I was easily exonerated of both, but the good officer never saw fit to apologize.

I sat up and swung my feet to the floor, surprised to see Mason glaring up at me from between them. Normally, he would have been sleeping next to me. "Couldn't sleep either, huh?"

He answered with a rattling in his chest and stalked from the room, tail held high.

I primed the coffee maker, showered, and dressed as fast as I could. Within twenty minutes I was in the Chrysler, thermal mug in hand.

Should have gotten up earlier. Who knew what Rarity would find? Maybe I should have insisted on getting her key and going over to check it out last night. Who was to say the thief would leave the salon in the same condition he had before? What if he'd trashed the place? What if Rarity walked in on something terrible?

I pressed harder on the accelerator and scooted through more than one intersection without stopping. After parking in front of the salon, I checked my watch before getting out. Six a.m. Earlier than I'd ever been there. Earlier than I'd ever been up.

All lights were on, and I could see through the window that the reception area and work spaces were in good condition. The shop appeared unoccupied, but I knew Rarity would be in the back room.

Pushing through the front door, I strode to the back. Rarity stood in the middle of the store room, with her hands on her hips.

She pointed to the almost bare shelves. "Look. You were right. I should have called the police the first time. It was my own silly pride that caused this."

She pulled up a stool and sat on it, propping her elbows on her knees.

I sipped my coffee, feeling a bit useless. "You called the police, right?"

"Yes, as soon as I got here, about half an hour ago. Maybe I'm getting too old to run a business. At first, I was afraid I'd been absent minded. You know, thought it was my age—or dementia. And then, I was certain it was kids, and I could take care of that easily enough. Now look. I'm out more money. My own fault." She stared at the vacant shelves.

My brain kicked in. "Rarity, it isn't your fault. Whoever did this, it's their fault. Why don't I make you some coffee?"

"Okay, sure." I did a double-take. The words didn't sound like Rarity's voice—much too breathy and resigned.

When the coffee pot began to fizz, I returned to the supply room. Rarity hadn't moved.

Encouragement had always been Rarity's forte, not mine. I dug deep into my memory to find some uplifting words. "Don't worry, Rarity. We'll discover who's behind this. Everything will be back to normal in no time at all. Um. This too will pass." That exhausted my full catalogue of encouragement.

Rarity managed a weak smile, not her usual ear to ear grin, but a smile nonetheless. "You're right. I'll just think about what I can learn from this. God lets things happen for a reason."

At her lowest point, Rarity's more encouraging than I am. I pulled up a stool to wait for the police.

Chapter Seven

The string of bells on the front door jingled, and I hurried to the waiting room to welcome the police. Of course, it was Officer Farlow, looking just like he did in my dream—standing straight as a board, starched uniform, with an equally stiff expression on his face. I expected to hear the words, "Halloren, you're under arrest."

Rarity poked her head out of the back room. "Oh, hi Jimmy. Come on back. I'll show you our little problem."

He strode away without acknowledging me. I took my place at the desk, picturing the man with his ever-present notebook, recording every word Rarity uttered.

About five minutes later, the sharp clip clop of footsteps signaled his approach. I put my pencil behind my ear and smiled up at Officer Farlow, when he stopped beside me.

"Ms. Halloren, Ms. Peabody tells me you saw someone enter the salon last night."

Crap, I knew this was coming.

"Yes I did. I was sitting in my car in the parking lot

across the street." I pointed. I don't know why. There was only one parking lot.

"And, what time was that?"

"Umm, probably about midnight."

"About midnight." He wrote it in his notebook before lifting his eyes to meet mine.

"Why were you out there at that hour?"

I didn't want to explain my brilliant idea of the stakeout and how it had proved ineffective, but forged ahead as simply as possible.

Thankfully, he didn't laugh, only stared at me for a moment. "Hmm. Quite a plan. Why didn't you call the station when you saw the break-in?"

I put my hand to my forehead to show I'd had only a momentary lapse in judgement. "I should have called, I know. I wish I had. But I wanted to talk to Rarity. She thought, and I did at one time, it was kids stealing hair color to use on themselves. She wanted to find out who it was, and talk to them herself. But then, last night I was pretty sure it wasn't kids. Looked like a man. Anyway, I left it up to Rarity."

Yikes, should have phrased that differently. Now I knew what it meant to throw someone under the bus. In my defense, I had to be truthful and confess everything. Besides, he'd be more forgiving of Rarity than of me. In my previous experience with Farlow, hedging the truth got me into deep trouble.

Rarity stepped up beside Farlow, full of her former vitality. "That's right, Jimmy. It was all my fault. Lauren wanted to inform the authorities even before last night, but I thought I could take care of it. So silly of me. I'm sorry I didn't call you."

Farlow nodded at Rarity. "No problem at all, Ms.

Peabody. I completely understand."

He leveled his gaze at me. "What exactly did you see, Ms. Halloren?"

I gave as detailed a report as I could, although it didn't sound like much. Dark clad figure, stocky. A second person in the car. The car was dark colored and looked like a four-door sedan. It had to be four doors because the first man put something in the back seat.

"So, there were two of them. One in the car and one who went inside? You thought they were adult? How did you come up with that assumption?"

"Well, I don't know for sure. I guess it was the way he moved. We just had the feeling it was an adult."

"You only saw one outside of the car. Is that correct?"

"Yes."

"So how do you know the person driving the car was not a teenager?"

"You're right. I don't know anything about that one. I only saw the one person, clearly. Or, not really clearly."

"And you said, "we." You gave me the impression you were alone. Who was with you?"

Crap, again.

"Oh. My friend, Anita, was with me. She wanted to keep me company in the sta—while I watched."

"Why didn't you mention your friend in the beginning?"

Because I wanted to protect her from Farlow's relentless scrutiny. Boy, I hated talking to law enforcement. On further thought, Anita wouldn't mind being questioned. She told me once she used to babysit Jimmy Farlow.

"I don't know why I didn't mention her, except she saw the same thing I saw, actually less than I did. She can't help you."

"I'll be the judge of whether she can help or not, Ms. Halloren." His voice oozed impatience. "What's her name?"

"Anita Corwin."

He recorded that in his notebook.

"What else do you remember about last night? Something you might have deemed unimportant."

"Nothing. There isn't anything else. That's all I can tell you, officer. The vehicle drove off without even turning on its lights, and when I attempted to follow, it disappeared."

Farlow looked up at the ceiling, and then he actually rolled his eyes. "Disappeared, huh? Like what, it was a ghost? It just up and disappeared. Or maybe like a figment of your vast imagination?"

I took a deep breath before allowing myself to answer. "No. I didn't imagine it. It disappeared. It must have turned down a street or an alley that I didn't see."

Farlow slapped his notebook shut, pivoted on his heel, and walked toward the door. With his back to us, he said, "Good day, ladies. Call me if you think of anything else you forgot to tell me—or didn't think important."

Rarity followed him to the door. "Thank you so much for coming so quickly. Bye, Jimmy."

After watching him get into his squad car, she turned to me with her hands on her hips. "Isn't Jimmy Farlow a nice young man? He sure has made something of himself. So conscientious and polite."

And I thought I was good at creative writing.

Rarity lived in a different world.

"Thank you for coming in, Lauren. You go on home now. So kind of you to be here. It isn't even your day to work."

She pushed her hair from her face and headed toward the supply room. "I'll call a locksmith right away and get the locks changed. What a bother."

Rarity seemed to have recovered nicely. I was happy to go home and forget about crime for a while. I grabbed my handbag. There was a time I dreamed of writing true crime novels, but the calling had lost its appeal. Experience kept telling me that particular genre was not my strong suit. Better to stay with my proven talent, writing mild travel articles, guaranteed to bore anyone under forty-five to death.

Chapter Eight

C at breath warmed my cheek. Round, golden eyes hovered two inches from my fluttering eyelids. "Good morning, Mason. What are you doing in my face? You've put on weight. Can't breathe with you on my chest."

My friendly feline leapt to the floor and loped out of the room as if on a mission. Rapping sounded on the front door before my feet hit the floor. That cat's got amazing hearing.

"Shoot, I forgot. And I'm late." I'd made a pact with my friend Clair. We'd get out and walk three mornings a week. It seemed like a really good idea at the time.

I peeked through the window to see Clair jogging in place on the front porch. She wore black-and-red flowered leggings, a red tank top, and matching sweatband.

As soon as I opened the door, she trotted in.

"Sorry, I missed my alarm." I hadn't set an alarm. I'm of the opinion anyone can set a mental alarm and be up on time. Obviously, it isn't a foolproof plan.

"Not a problem, girlfriend. I'm early. Couldn't wait to get our exercise program underway." She assessed my attire, over-sized t-shirt, sweat pants, and bed head. "You get dressed. I'll make coffee and feed Mason."

"Thanks." Friends since high school, Clair's age was the same as mine. Where did she get her energy?

I slouched off to the bedroom to dig out better quality sweats and drag a comb through my hair.

Clair maintained a conversation from the kitchen. "How's Rarity doing now? Have the police come up with anything?"

"Nope. I'm pretty sure the police department doesn't consider stolen hair products a priority. We haven't heard from them in a few days. But Rarity is fine. Back to her old cheerful self."

I tied my shoes in rhythm to Clair's pep talk from the kitchen. "Now that we're in our forties, we have to be intentional about staying in shape. And as a writer, you spend far too much time in a chair. Your job at Rarity's beauty shop isn't any better. You're at that reception desk all day."

The lovely aroma of fresh coffee pulled me to the kitchen. Clair placed a steaming mug into my hands.

"I don't sit all day at the salon, only four hours in the morning. And I walk to and from work, when the weather's good." *Sometimes.*

"That's not enough activity to keep anybody fit. Swallow that coffee and let's get on the road." Clair bounced around my kitchen like a prizefighter, while I made an attempt to enjoy the one cup of caffeine I'd be allowed before we set out.

Too soon, Clair was pointing at the door, and I

followed her down the concrete steps.

She launched into a fast-paced walk. "Come on, girlfriend. Let's get that blood pumping. Don't you love fresh morning air? This is the perfect time to power walk. Sets the pace for the whole day. Extra fat will melt away."

There'd never been an extra ounce of fat on that body of hers.

I struggled to keep pace, ejecting words as I was able, between breaths. "Not so sure I love it. But...I know...good for me."

"Wait until you see this walking path. It winds through the woods, along the stream, and there's a beautiful ravine up ahead. So peaceful." She pumped her arms and picked up the pace.

With a deep breath, I completed two entire sentences. "Great. What's this got to do with peaceful? Will there be a place to sit?"

Clair powered up a hill and turned onto a tree-lined walkway. It was beautiful, or I think it was, if I'd had time to take it in. I scanned the vegetation in a vain attempt to appreciate nature, but returned to eyes front just in time to keep from slamming into Clair. She'd stopped.

"Someone threw a gum wrapper on the ground. How careless." Clair bent over and picked up the silvery bit of paper and stuffed it into her pocket. "Such a shame. Our trails are among the nicest in the state. People don't appreciate what the city council has done for us." She was on the march again.

I wanted to be cheerful and made every effort between gulps of oxygen. "Love the trees. Stream would be peaceful. Wish we could stop and look."

"I knew you'd love it. We can't stop yet. We just got our heart rates up."

Why wasn't she out of breath? I decided to fore-go conversation, and concentrate on my stride.

Once again, Clair abruptly applied the brakes. I was three steps past her before I managed to stop.

She spun around and pointed into the trees. "Look down there in the valley." Her hands dropped to her hips. "Somebody left a bunch of trash."

Following her glare, I could see it. A pile of rags had been tossed down the hill. They were almost hidden among weeds and dry leaves.

Clair steamed off down the walk, faster than before. "Some people are so inconsiderate. Remind me to get a garbage bag when we get to your place, and I'll come back to pick that up."

I broke into a trot to catch up. "Really? You're coming back to pick up trash?" Of course, she would. Clair was insanely civic-minded.

After thirty minutes of agony, on my part, Stoneybridge Drive came into view. My little Cape Cod never looked so inviting. Visions of steaming coffee gave me renewed energy for the last block. Finally, I trudged up the steps and leaned into the door until it opened.

I swear I could see electricity sparking from Clair as she jogged to the kitchen. "Do you have a garbage bag? We've got to go back to pick up that rubbish."

"We? Now? Don't you want to sit down and have a cup of coffee first? How about a bottle of water?"

"No. We can't just leave it there. A black mark on the community. Everyone using the trails will have to look at it."

Why did she keep saying "we"? I cast a longing gaze at the cold coffee maker and pulled a black plastic bag from the cupboard. Clair grabbed it and tucked it into her waistband while she marched out the front door.

"Come on, Lauren. We'll have this done in no time." She set off at a rapid clip toward the woods.

Mason peeked from under the dining table, and our eyes met, as I pulled the door shut behind me, then mustered my strength and set off to follow Clair.

I lost sight of her during the last leg of the trek. Catching my breath at the top of the hill, I scanned the area. Clair wasn't in sight. I ventured to other side of the walk and peered into the ravine. There she was, clinging to the embankment, already halfway to the bottom.

She shouted up at me. "Why would anyone climb all the way down here, through the trees and weeds, just to throw garbage away?"

I wondered why anyone would climb all the way down there to pick it up.

Still ranting, Clair steadily made her way to the bottom. "It would have been easier to find a public trash bin. Some people go out of their way to break the law."

I found a sturdy tree trunk on which to lean as I watched her descent. "Be careful. There's no need to rush. That stuff isn't going anywhere."

Clair skidded the last few feet to bottom of the slope, and made her way to the pile. I had to chuckle watching her arms flail when she ran into a swarm of flies.

I did admire her. She always thought of the good of

the town.

Kicking leaves aside, Clair opened the garbage bag and reached to grasp a crumpled red cloth. All of a sudden, her hand flew open and jerked back to her chest. An odd wail seemed to emanate from deep inside her as she straightened, eyes still riveted to the pile of rags.

"What's going on?" I strained to see what held her attention. "Clair, what are you doing? Are you going to pick up that stuff so we can go home? I still need coffee."

That's when her scream pierced the air, and my blood froze. Clair spun around to gape at me, mouth open wide, but now releasing no sound at all. I cocked my head and peered back at her, still unable to discern what the commotion was about.

After a final glance at the ground, she began a frantic—almost comical—struggle up the slope. More than once, she lost her footing and slid back, then grasped at small trees and bushes to pull herself forward.

She neared the top and I offered my hand to pull her up the last few steps. "Did you see a snake?" I began to laugh, but another look at her eyes stifled it.

She gained her footing on the trail and maintained the grip on my hand, which was beginning to tingle from lack of circulation. Clair stared straight at me, eyes wide, mouth open, mute. She lifted her other hand and pointed at the trash.

"What? Clair, what's the matter?" I began prying her fingers loose, one at a time.

Finally finding her voice, she uttered, "Body. Dead person. Call 911."

"Dead person?" I turned my attention to the pile of leaves and rubbish, while I dug my hand into my pocket to find my cell.

My mind spun as I punched in the three digits. Simplifying the emergency number had to have been the best idea ever.

"Hello? Um, my friend found the body of a person in the ravine along the walking path." I stumbled with the words. Too bad there wasn't a three-number code for "dead person, send help".

"A body? Is this person breathing?"

"Um. I don't think so. Clair, were they breathing?"

Clair grabbed the phone from my hand. "Hello, my name is Clair Lane. I'm on the walking path between Maple Street and Juniper Avenue. I found the body. It's down in the ravine. They're dead, I'm sure. I couldn't tell whether it's a man or a woman and I'm pretty sure they've been there a while."

While Clair finished her call, I wandered to the other side of the path and found a place to sit on the ground.

Clair clicked the phone off and sat beside me. "It's okay. They're sending someone right away."

I looked at Clair, but couldn't think of anything to say. We sat in silence.

Within minutes sirens signaled the approach of the EMS and probably a police car. Soon, a cluster of first responders and two men carrying a stretcher between them jogged toward us.

Chapter Nine

An intricate network of ropes snaked down into the ravine, linking trees at the top to those at the foot. A medic attached the stretcher and crates of supplies to the ropes, then carefully lowered them to the bottom. Two of his coworkers broke from the crowd hovering around the body to retrieve the supplies. Clair and I clung to each other at the top of the hill, unable to tear our attention away from the scene.

We were so intent on the activity that a sharp voice caused both of us to jump. "Halloren? What'd you do now? Do you follow trouble around, or does it follow you?"

I turned to find Officer Farlow standing behind us. His eyes burrowed into mine.

Geez. Just what I needed. Stony-faced and stern, Farlow lived and breathed regulations. Did he ever smile?

"I didn't do anything." My hand took on a life of its own and pointed at Clair. "She found a body." As a writer, you would think I'd come up with a more articulate answer.

"Hmmm." He maintained eye contact while deftly opening that aggravating notebook. "What were you two doing out here this morning?"

"Walking."

"Why?"

"Exercise." *How many writers do you know who can't string two words together in a sentence? It's a good thing I landed the part-time receptionist job.*

"You were out for exercise, so what were you doing in the ravine? Let me guess. You've taken up mountain climbing." *I think he almost cracked a smile at his little joke.*

Again, I pointed to Clair. "She went down there."

Farlow released me from his gaze and turned the spotlight on my friend. "And your name is?"

"Clair Lane. I'm a real estate agent here in Evelynton. I'm sure you've seen my signs around town. Top-dollar producer last year. I don't have a business card with me, but I'll get you one." *She had obviously recovered from the horrific experience of discovering a corpse.*

"Ms. Lane, why did you leave the walkway and go down into the gully?"

Clair launched into a short, but forceful, discourse on the disposal of refuse on public property, finishing with, "I thought someone had thrown their garbage down there, so I took a plastic bag and climbed down to pick it up, as is my civic duty."

She raised an index finger. "By the way, that black plastic bag is the one I left there. It isn't part of the evidence. Well, as you can see, I discovered the trash wasn't rags at all, but clothes attached to a body."

"Yes ma'am. Did you recognize the victim?"

"How would I recognize it? I don't even know if it's a man or a woman. There's no face. Just a bloody mess with flies crawling all over it."

My vision became a little blurry. Trees swirled around me, my knees buckled, and I sank to the ground. Clair hadn't shared that disturbing information with me. A vivid imagination can be a curse. Propping my head between my knees slowed the swirl, and I began to breathe again.

While I stared at the dirt, I heard the snap of Farlow's notebook snapped shut and he stepped away.

"I'll be in touch with you both. You'll need to come downtown to issue and sign a formal statement later today." When his footsteps retreated a bit further, I glanced up to find him staring at me.

"Do you want someone to drive you home, Ms. Halloren?"

Clair spoke for me. "No. We're fine. We'll walk."

Gee, thanks Clair. I guessed her legs were a lot steadier than mine.

Chapter Ten

One forty-five, the perfect time of day at Ava's Java. The business lunch crowd was its way back to work, and the late afternoon coffee drinkers hadn't arrived.

I could only describe Ava as a robust woman with an athletic build. She towered over me by about four inches. "Hi Lauren. How are you? Haven't had a chance to talk to you since the excitement. A dead body?" She handed me my light roast coffee with low-fat milk. I came in so often, she knew what I liked. That made me smile. That she catalogued all the town gossip, and wanted to talk about it, I didn't so much.

I took a deep breath, prepared to offer the short version. "Yeah, I…"

Ava's phone rang, and she swiveled to grab it, saving me from having to continue.

I weaved my way through empty tables to the sunny spot by the window and snuggled into the chair across from Anita. Then I took a long slow drink.

Anita placed a bookmark in her paperback and glanced up. "Isn't this a great day? I have the whole afternoon with nothing to do."

"That sounds heavenly. I could use a little relaxation after these last crazy couple of weeks. The robberies. Ugh, the body." I put a hand over my eyes, trying to shut out the image.

"Well at least we can forget about solving the robberies, since Rarity reported them. And that poor dead person. The police said it was a man, didn't they? People are saying it had to be a transient. I bet they'll discover he wandered into town and died of a heart attack or something."

"They confirmed it was a man, but that's all so far. Clair's description didn't indicate a natural death, but who am I to say? I guess anything could have happened after he died. Anyway, I'd love to get back to peaceful small-town life, with nothing to worry about other than feeding my cat."

My gaze wandered to the street. "What the…"

I turned back to Anita and stared at her for a minute before I formed the words. "Um. I must be seeing things. The motorcycle that just went by. Did you see it?"

Anita looked up from her coffee. "No. I heard it, I think. Why?"

"There was woman riding on the back. She was wearing a skirt and heels. I'd almost think it was Clair."

Anita laughed out loud. "Sure, Clair on a motorcycle. Can you just imagine it? Drink up. I think you need more caffeine. Clair's crazy, but not that crazy."

"You're right. She wouldn't ride one, even in jeans. Does she own a pair of jeans?"

Anita cocked her head and shrugged. "Not to my knowledge."

"Well, the woman on the bike was wearing a helmet so I couldn't see her face, and she was going pretty fast."

I sipped my coffee and thought about what I would do if I had no responsibilities for a whole day.

Anita drew my attention back to reality. "Has Rarity heard anything from the police yet?"

"Nothing. To tell you the truth, I don't think our police force has any desire to investigate the theft. Probably haven't even thought about it. They don't think it's important enough."

"Too bad. I suppose they have enough to keep them busy. And maybe Rarity was right in the beginning. It might have been kids."

I returned to my peaceful thoughts, telling myself to let it go. Forget the hair color mystery and the dead person in the gully. And I'd almost reached that serene place when Anita exclaimed, "Oh my."

"Hmm?" I looked up at Anita. Her mouth hung open, and her eyes focused over my right shoulder. I shifted in my chair to discover this new object of interest.

Clair stepped through the entry of the coffee shop. The door swung closed behind her as she moved in our direction. After a wave to Ava, a secret signal between the two of them, meaning she needed coffee, Clair pulled out a chair at our table and sank into it with a thunk. She took a deep breath and fiddled with her purse.

I stared at her, trying to arrange my perspective, and adjust the tone of my voice, before putting my thoughts into words.

With unusual restraint, Anita began. "Hi, Clair. How's it going?"

"Fine." Clair's voice was faint. Talk about unusual.

My mind was still busy taking in Clair's appearance. "Um, new hairstyle?" Could have been more creative with the question.

She cut her eyes to me. Her lips formed a little O, before both hands flew to her head. She felt what we saw—hair that looked like it had been ironed flat and glued to her head. Clair began a poking and lifting motion. Then she bent over and scrubbed at her head. When she righted herself, her hair resembled her signature spiky style.

Anita gave up on restraint and tact. "Girl, what in the world happened to you? You're a wreck."

Clair straightened and raised her chin. "I had a date."

"What?" That question was a duet from Anita and me.

"You know, I told you I joined that online dating site. I met a new guy today. He was nice, and so proud of his motorcycle."

Anita interrupted. "A motorcycle? Clair, you can't be serious. He wouldn't be a match for you. You don't like motorcycles, do you?"

"No, I don't, but he's cute. Besides, eight out of ten guys on the site ride them. What's with men over forty and motorcycles? Anyway, I decided to go with it." She adjusted a strand of hair. "I'm up for new adventures."

Ava arrived with coffee, which Clair accepted with both hands. She took a big slurp before continuing.

"He said it'd be a short ride. He said he'd take it easy. He said we'd see the sights and I'd love it." She closed her eyes and put a hand to her forehead.

Anita took a sip of her own coffee. "So you didn't love it?"

"If that was taking it easy, I never want to be on a hard ride. I couldn't see the scenery, because I had my eyes shut. At least I was sitting in back, so he blocked most of the bugs." She glanced down at her jacket and brushed off a few specks. One of which crawled away after it hit the floor.

"He just kept going and going. We must have been on every dirt road in the county. I started to think I'd been kidnapped. Then he slowed enough that I opened my eyes and saw the blessed city limit sign. Finally got back to the restaurant. I've never been so glad to crawl into my car. It felt like I was being hugged by my momma."

Clair shuddered and straightened her shoulders. "Enough about that. What's going on with the missing products at The Rare Curl?"

I had more questions about her date, such as—did he want a goodbye kiss, but thought better of it.

"Nothing. I think the police have already filed it away. But it's okay because there hasn't been any trouble since Rarity had the locks changed."

"Good. Maybe Rarity was right, and it was kids who've moved on to something new. Probably done messing with their hair."

"Hope so. I'm not sure even kids should get away with theft, but if Rarity's happy...."

I glanced at the time on my phone. "Well girls, I have to get over to the nursing home. Louise is expecting me." I gathered my coffee mug and napkin and slid my chair out.

Anita rested her chin on her palm. "I know you said you got yourself into doing that article by mistake, but you're really enjoying it, aren't you?"

"I am. Sweet Louise really looks forward to our chats. You know the article is about the residents who never have visitors. I knew it was a problem, but talking to those lovely old people has really brought it home. They're lonely, but they never complain. And they're so appreciative of any attention I give them."

"Maybe you have a new ministry." Anita was into ministry, always looking to help the less fortunate.

"I don't know about that. It's sort of time consuming. I'll see you girls later. I want to finish the article tonight and get it submitted. The newspaper won't pay much, but it'll be something." I deposited my cup on the counter on my way out.

Would my writing ever be more interesting than, "Nursing Home Tidbits"?

Chapter Eleven

The sign read *Beaver Creek Resident and Rehabilitation Center*.

I really had to lose the habit of referring to it as the nursing home. None of the residents wanted to think of it in that way.

I'd become accustomed to the sterile, medication-scented, air that hit me in the face as I opened the door. The usual group of residents, manning wheelchairs and walkers, were stationed to greet me. Not just me— anyone who happened to come in.

"Hello, Edward." He never spoke, but liked to stand very close to each new arrival. I wondered if he was nearsighted as I nudged him back a couple steps in order to close the door.

How're you doing today, Mildred?" She smiled and stared at a point just left of my face.

None of the greeters, as I'd begun to call them, knew me. I'd introduced myself several times before I realized that every day was a new experience for them.

I edged my way through the old-timers, waved at the receptionist, who did remember me. Louise

Humphreys' room was in the first hallway to the right. At ninety, her mind was still intact. She had a pretty good command of history. Her short-term memory wasn't so good, but long-term was great. During our last conversation, she'd fallen asleep in the middle of a particularly exciting tale. I thought the story would make a great finale for my article, once I heard the ending.

A nurse I didn't recognize stood beside Louise in her room, so I stopped at her open door and tapped on the frame.

As she removed a blood pressure cuff, the nurse glanced at me. "Come on in. We're all finished."

Louise's face crinkled into a grin. "Lauren, this is my new nurse, Paula. She transferred here from the Rehab Center in Warrenton. Paula, my friend Lauren's a writer."

Paula smiled at me, then turned back to Louise. "You're doing fine. Give me a call if you start to worry again. I'm here until six." She gathered her equipment and passed me in the doorway.

Louise occupied a massive, green arm chair—a size too large for her small frame.

"Lauren, it's so good to see you."

"I'm glad to see you, too. Are you feeling okay?"

She patted her hair and blushed. "Well, Paula said I'm fine, so I must be. Felt like my heart was going to beat right out of my chest a little while ago. It's better now."

Louise inclined her head toward the room across the hall. "Probably because of my neighbor. Deloris was up all night, and her cackling kept me awake."

"Cackling? What was causing that?" I tried to

picture what that meant. Maybe a chicken clucking?

"Oh, she's got a computer in there, and she runs some sort of business. Every time she makes a sale she laughs out loud or claps her hands or shouts. You'd think that woman was making a million dollars. I doubt an old lady like her could earn much. I wonder if she's even allowed to have a business in here. But I don't say anything to the staff."

"This doesn't happen all the time, does it? Keeping you up?"

"Nope. She's not usually so loud. Or if I wake up, I have to go to the bathroom anyway. Last night was the worst. It went on for hours."

"It's interesting, a business in the nursing home. Um, in Beaver Creek. I bet it helps to pass the time. I'd love to hear about it. Do you think she'd tell me about it?"

"Oh, that woman would brag about it to anyone. Probably would talk your leg off. She loves having her own income. Come on, I'll take you over." Louise eased off the chair and began to shuffle from the room. At the door, she paused and checked the hall in each direction before starting across.

I suppose speeding wheel chairs might be a danger if you're ninety.

We crossed the hall holding hands, me matching shuffle for shuffle. I'd learned this mode of transportation since meeting Louise.

The black-and-white name plate with little flowers in the corners read Deloris D'agostino.

Louise tapped on the door and shuffled in. "Hey Deloris, I brought someone to meet you."

The room was identical to Louise's, but Mrs.

D'agostino packed a lot more into it. Along the far wall sat a single bed, covered in a bright red comforter. At the foot, a mobility scooter, complete with basket on the front, was plugged into a wall outlet. A large flowered recliner, occupied the space to the left of the bed, and a smaller matching chair snuggled next to that. To our right, a shorter wall held a closet and the bathroom door. To our left, as we entered, the wall was monopolized by a massive dresser and mirror.

In the center of the room, a large woman perched on an undersized desk chair, in front of a small desk. She busily tapped on a laptop computer.

"Deloris, this is my friend, Lauren."

Deloris was as round as she was tall. Her startling black hair was pulled back in a bun, showing an inch of extremely white roots.

The woman glanced up from the computer screen, and smiled broadly. "Come see what good business I'm doing, Louise. I have thirty-five auctions running all at the same time. And half of them will be paying off by dinnertime. I'm having so much fun, I can't stand it."

"Good for you, Deloris." Louise didn't put as much enthusiasm in the remark as I might have. "In fact, that's why we're here. Lauren is a writer, and she wants to hear about your business."

Deloris tore her attention away from the screen. "I've seen you around. You're writing the newspaper article about the old people nobody wants to visit." She cut her eyes to her neighbor. "Sorry Louise."

She pointed to the computer screen. "Anyway, let me tell you. I have my own store. My son Mallozi—who visits me every day—set it up for me on this auction site. I monitor the sales, collect the money, and email my buyers. That's the best part. Some of them are from other countries. It's very interesting."

Deloris grabbed the sides of the desk and studied the computer screen for a moment. "They're bidding like crazy."

"I'm fascinated, Deloris. What do you sell?"

Deloris pursed her lips for a moment. Her eyes narrowed. "Oh. Um, odds and ends my son finds at garage sales and such. He keeps all the stuff at home. Wouldn't have room here." Deloris eyed me as she spoke. With one hand, she slowly closed the laptop.

She clasped her hands in her lap. "Mallozi tells me I talk about it too much. Someone might cut in to my business and sell the same stuff."

"I promise I wouldn't do that. It must be exciting to run a business and earn your own income. Do you share the proceeds with Mallozi?"

"I give him a cut, sure. There's plenty of money for both of us. He'll be here shortly to load pictures of my next batch."

"It wouldn't fit in my current article, but I'd love to do a follow-up piece and interview you about your business. You wouldn't have to say anything about what you sell. I can see it keeps you busy and I bet it gives you quite a sense of accomplishment."

"Oh yes. I'd never worked in my life, except for keeping house and raising kids. Now I'm an executive. Sometimes I even eat in my room so I can watch my auctions. It's great." Deloris's smile fled and she glanced to the side. "But I don't think I should be in the newspaper. Mallozi doesn't like publicity. He's a private person."

She brushed some imaginary dust off the top of the

computer. "It's not that interesting. Nothing really, just a little thing I do to pass the time."

What caused the quick change in Deloris? She didn't seem to be one of the memory care residents.

A knock on the door interrupted us. A man stepped into the room. He was about my height, a lot bulkier, and in need of a shave. "Hey, Ma. How's it going?"

Deloris's face brightened. "Mallozi. Come in and meet my friends."

She turned glowing eyes to me. "This is my son, Mallozi. I told you he'd be here. Like clockwork, he's here every day to check on me and make sure I have everything I need. Don't you sweetie?"

"Sure do. I take care of my ma. Wouldn't have it any other way."

Mallozi crossed in front of me to kiss his mother on the cheek. When he straightened, he spread his hands, narrowing his gaze at Louise and me. "What did I break up, ladies?"

Deloris spoke up. "Nothing much. Lauren is a newspaper writer. She's writing a story about the old folks who live here and don't have any wonderful children like you. The ones who don't have anyone to visit them. Poor things." She shot a glance at Louise.

Her son eyed me for a few seconds before a smile lifted his face. "That's real nice of you. But you aren't interviewing my mom, are you? As she said, she's got me. I'm here every day."

Louise shuffled to my side and put her tiny hand my arm. "Oh no, Mallozi, I brought Lauren over to meet Deloris and show her the business. We all know Deloris is one of the lucky ones with such a dutiful son."

"Your mother must have a good business sense. I'm amazed she's so productive, even while living in assisted care. It's quite an accomplishment."

He nodded and continued to eye me.

Louise was tugging on my arm, so I took the hint. "We were just leaving. I know you'll want to have your visit. So glad I met you, Deloris, and you, Mallozi."

Louise and I shuffled out the door and back across the hall.

When we reached her room, I whispered. "I don't think Deloris's son appreciated me visiting her."

"Oh, you know boys. He was probably in a mood, and he's a little possessive. Sort of wants all her attention, but it's lovely he makes time for her."

Louise took her place in the big green chair, and I sat on the edge of the bed.

I took out my notebook. "Now, about that story you were telling me last week. The one about you and your brother trying to stow away on the train? I can't wait to hear how it turned out."

As much as I enjoyed Louise, I was glad to leave Beaver Creek. I trotted to the parking lot filling my lungs with glorious, non-medicated air.

My hand had just gripped the door handle when I heard the footsteps. I glanced up to see Mallozi stalking toward my car.

Where had he come from? I'd assumed he was still with Deloris. Had he been sitting on the bench in the little park nearby?

Mallozi closed in, and I wondered if I should jump out of the way. He finally stopped with his face about six inches from mine. His damp breath on my face made me attempt to back up, but I was trapped between Mallozi and the car.

This man had no concept of personal space. I held my breath to keep from inhaling his recycled air.

His whisper sounded like a dog's growl. "That's a commendable thing you're doing for Louise and the old people. Nice."

He glanced from side to side before returning his gaze to me. "But I don't think you need to talk to my mom anymore. She has me to look after her, and she sure doesn't need to be bothered by any newspaper reporter."

"I'm not a reporter, I'm..."

Without another word, Mallozi pivoted and walked away.

I gulped a full breath. What was that about?

Shaking my shoulders to get rid of the creepy feeling, I yanked the car door open. Once inside, my trembling hand missed the ignition. Taking a deep calming breath, I concentrated and tried again, this time with success.

In the few blocks to my house, I must have checked the rear-view mirror twenty times. The streets were quiet. No one followed me.

Secure in my living room, with the door bolted, I laughed at such paranoia. The guy simply wanted to protect his mother. An admirable quality. He couldn't help being weird. Probably harmless.

Chapter Twelve

The three of us occupied a booth at Burgers & Bean Sprouts, a trendy little restaurant, housed inside a refurbished sixties-era filling station.

Clair shoved her plate to the center of the table.

Anita stopped in mid-bite. "Girl, you only ate half your sandwich, and you've barely touched those curly fries."

"No more for me. Can't even look at it. I've been eating way too much since joining the dating site." A smile crossed Clair's face. "Guess I shouldn't complain, I've had some great meals. All the guys are out to impress me." She gave her middle a pat. "But, it's beginning to show. Lauren, when are we going speed walking again?"

I'd hoped Clair had given it up. "I've barely recovered from our last walk. I'm still having nightmares. Maybe if we stay away from the woods?"

"Sure. But I doubt we'll find another body. I think Evelynton's hit its limit for the year."

Anita dabbed the corners of her mouth with her napkin. "Clair, you haven't put on an ounce since high school. Skinny then. Skinny now."

I wanted to echo the sentiment, but my mouth was full. My turkey burger, smothered with sautéed onions and bean sprouts, was the best thing I'd eaten in weeks. Dining out anywhere was a treat for me.

Clair blew out a loud sigh. "Guess I'll have to stop responding to every flirt message a man sends me. Or maybe, I'll cancel my membership, since I ran into an old acquaintance a couple days ago."

I watched Clair's smile expand into a grin that crinkled her eyes, and had to ask. "Who did you see?"

She twirled her straw in her lemonade. "I was in Indianapolis on business, and a certain someone with smoldering eyes and a dangerous edge happened to be there."

Anita made no attempt to hide the rolling of her eyes. "Who did you meet this time?"

"Mr. Tall Dark and Gorgeous. Remember the FBI agent, Jack Spencer? He was in Evelynton when that insurance agent, Earl Clooney, was killed. You know, he was chasing Philip Townsend, the jerk I dated a few times. You remember Agent Spencer, don't you, Lauren?"

I remembered him very well. But for Clair, I put on my best impersonation of disinterested. "Sure. He came into The Rare Curl during the investigation."

I'd thought about him many times since he left town. The first man I'd had a crush on since Marc died. Jack was just as Clair described him. I could add warm, strong, and sincere.

And I needed to jump off that train of thought right away. A relationship wasn't meant to be. The last time I'd gazed into those dark eyes, I'd slammed a door in

Jack Spencer's handsome face. He'd made the mistake of voicing suspicions about my late husband. Insinuated Marc had been involved in a crime, before being killed by the stray bullet six years ago.

Clair went on, unaware of my darkened mood. "I thought Jack was gone forever, but spotted him in a coffee shop when I was in the city for a realtor meeting. Isn't that funny? The first time I laid eyes on him was in Ava's Java, when he'd stopped in for coffee. We already have something special going for us."

Anita pointed a french fry. "I remember. Aren't you glad you were already finished with that Townsend character when Agent Spencer told you he was a criminal? I thought the agent went back to Florida."

"He did." Clair's expression went all dreamy. "But now he's living in Indiana."

I fought to sound casual. "What's he doing in Indiana?"

"I didn't have a chance to get the whole story. He was with some other guys. I just said 'hello' and introduced myself to make sure he remembered me. He did say I don't have to call him agent anymore. He retired and formed his own company. Security consulting, I think."

Clair picked up one of Anita's French fries and stuck in her mouth. There's another realtor motivational meeting in Indianapolis this weekend. I hadn't planned attend, but I sure will now. I may have to camp out in the coffee shop until Jack comes in again."

Former Agent Jack Spencer didn't stand a chance. Once Clair set her sights on a guy—well, she knew how to flirt. He'd be hooked and in the net before he knew what was happening.

Shoot.

I massaged my jaw where a pain had begun to creep in. Clenched teeth, a dead giveaway for jealousy. Something I hadn't experienced since high school.

This wasn't Clair's fault, she didn't know. I'd always been private about my feelings. Hadn't even admitted it to myself, until now. My friend didn't know I had feelings for him.

Clair slapped both hands on the table. "Girls! What was I thinking? When I see Jack, I'll tell him about my dreadful experience of finding the body alongside the path. And I'll ask his advice on how to get over the trauma."

She batted her eyelashes and did a passable imitation of a southern belle. "You know, Jack, I just don't feel safe anymore. I'm afraid to be alone." With a satisfied smile, Clair said, "Manly men can't help but offer assistance to a damsel in distress."

Damsel in distress? That woman was as independent as they came. Besides, her apartment building had more bolt locks and security cameras than anyone should need in a small town.

I picked up the last bit of turkey burger, but couldn't put it in my mouth. My appetite was gone. When I saw the waitress walking in our direction, I held up my plate for her to take.

Anita finished her last curly fry and wiped her fingers on the napkin. "This was great. Thanks for coming out at the last minute. I'd forgotten my hubby was going to be out of town, and I hate to eat alone."

Determined to get out of a foul mood that was creeping in, I sat up straighter. "It was perfect timing for me. Beaver Creek has a party scheduled for the residents in their new community room. It's called Evelyn's Party Room. Kind of cute, isn't it?"

Clair finished the last drop of her lemonade. "I've been watching the construction over there. They've added a whole new wing of rooms, haven't they?"

"They inherited money for the addition from a previous resident. It's the funniest story. Did you know Evelynton once had a different name?"

"What?" Clair gazed at me. "No way. And I would know, with my connection to real estate."

Anita laughed. "You should spend more time with the senior citizens of Evelynton. They love to talk about it."

She warmed to her subject. "It was originally named Craughville, after the founder and first mayor of the town, Jeremiah Craugh."

Clair groaned. "Ugh. I'm glad they changed it. How would you like to tell people, 'I'm from Craughville'? So, how'd they come up with Evelynton?"

Anita leaned in. "I guess Jeremiah's wife developed a serious case of empty-nest syndrome when their kids grew up. She started nagging her husband to do something to make her feel fulfilled. Guess what her name was? Evelyn. The only way Jeremiah was going to have any peace was to give her the town. Rumor is, they first renamed it Evelyn's Town, and it gradually became Evelynton."

I laughed. "And the moral to that story is, if you want something, nag. Have you heard this part? Fast forward something like a hundred years, and one of Evelyn Craugh's descendants moved into Beaver Creek. When she died, she left them a chunk of money in her will for additional resident rooms and a big activities room. She was adamant that the activities room be named Evelyn's Party Room. And she wanted it to be next to the pond. You know that little puddle is a ways from the original building, so they put resident rooms and hallways in between."

Clair leaned back in her seat. "I drove by the construction and wondered what in the world they were doing. The building meanders all over the property."

"The new resident rooms aren't finished yet, but they're christening Evelyn's Party Room tonight. There's a little musical group coming to entertain. Louise is so excited. She wanted me to be there as her date. I have just enough time to make it."

I slid out of the booth. "Night, girls. I'm off to a deliriously exciting night of toe-tapping with the over-eighty set."

The contrast between my night life and Clair's gave me a headache. *Wouldn't mind a little excitement, but what could happen at a nursing home?*

Chapter Thirteen

I punched in the code and pushed through the doors of Beaver Creek. No welcoming committee. Everyone would be at the party in the far side of the building. I'd been down these corridors when Helen gave me the tour of the new construction, but tonight the meandering halls were shrouded in an eerie silence. No old people shuffling along, no call-button beeps or television noise. Just quiet—and the sound of my own breathing. I walked on until the faint notes of a barber shop quartet told me Evelyn's Party Room was near.

I scanned the crowd from the doorway, searching for the tiny woman with fluffy white hair, among the other cotton-haired women of various sizes.

Deloris stood out with her black hair. Not many wore hair color, and none as dark as hers. She waved from her table near the stage, where she sat beside Mallozi. He turned a scowling face to me and returned his attention to the singers.

Hmmm. Friendly guy.

Susan, one of the younger aides, stepped over to me. "Hi, Lauren. Louise went back to her room. She wanted to use her own bathroom before we start the chair dance."

"What kind of dance did you say?"

"They chair dance, because most of them aren't too steady on their feet. It's like dancing, only sitting. They wave their hands and tap their feet. Louise would love it if you'd join in."

"I might do that. I can't be much worse at chair dancing than I am on my feet."

Susan checked her watch. "Louise has been gone long enough. She's probably fine, but would you mind checking on her? She insisted she could go on her own, and she had her walker. I have to stay here and help with the others."

I muttered to myself. "Why would you let a ninety-year old woman go all that way on her own?"

Susan didn't hear because she was carrying it across the room. "I'll set this at Louise's table for you."

"Sure. Thanks."

Okay, I'd power walk back to the other side of the building. Maybe I'd count it as exercise. Clair would be proud.

I rounded the last corner to find Louise standing in her doorway. Her little head turned to peer down the hall, one way and then the other.

"Are you okay, Louise?"

"Oh Lauren, I'm so glad to see you. It's that darn walker. I got it stuck behind my recliner. Could you pull the pesky thing out for me?"

"Of course, I will." Muttering to myself again, about neglectful staff, I yanked the walker free and positioned it in front of Louise.

Together we shuffled the vacant halls. Louise told me about her day. She had a painting class—finished a flower picture. She wasn't thrilled with the dessert they served with lunch. She thought pineapple was an odd flavor for Jell-O.

Soon the rousing harmony of male voices echoed through the corridor, and we walked into the party at full swing.

Louise sang along and swayed to the tunes. Personally, a couple rounds of "Ain't Misbehavin'" and "Frog Kissin'" were plenty. I was getting antsy.

The nurses began moving chairs to the center of the floor, preparing for more fun. Louise clapped her hands and looked at me. "Oh, we're going to dance. This is fun. You'll love it."

"Louise, I'll want to take a picture with my phone, but I must have left my handbag in your room. I'll be right back."

Louise flashed me a smile and a wave. I slipped out, looking forward to the solitude.

Trekking the vacant halls, I soaked in the tranquility, until everything went black.

Crap.

Someone had accidentally hit the light switch. I stood still and waited for them to realize their error. It remained pitch black.

I made an effort to help them recognize the mistake. "Hello? Excuse me. Did someone turn off the light?"

No response.

The minutes ticked by. My voice squeaked. "Hello?"

With a deep breath I fought to remain calm. Was there a motion detector to conserve energy? I jumped up and down and waved my arms. Nothing happened.

Thinking on that, a motion detector didn't make sense anyway. Some of the residents didn't move enough to keep it activated. The power would be flipping off all the time.

After about two more minutes, I finally accepted the hallway would remain dark. So, stretching out my arms in front of me, I shuffled on. Since I'd been this way three times that evening, I was fairly confident of the path.

Oh, thank goodness. A light shone in the next corridor up ahead, so I let it draw me forward, ignoring the butterflies in my stomach.

I was almost there, ready to be in the light, when it extinguished. I stopped short. Everything was pitch black again.

Crap.

There must be some explanation for this bizarre event. Maybe an overly enthusiastic orderly or janitor.

"Hello?" I spoke in an elevated, but non-hysterical voice. "Would you turn on a light, please? I know you thought everyone was out of this area. I'm sorry to make extra work, but I'm on my way to pick up my handbag from a resident's room."

The only reply was a squeak of rubber-soled shoes in the distance. The aide was probably irritated at having to return to the control panel. I waited, but there were only more distant footsteps.

Now the fear approached paralysis level. I fought to tamp it down, but my heart pounded harder. With mincing steps, I edged forward with one hand on the wall until I reached what I thought should be the corner. I needed to turn, but which way? Funny how I could be so disoriented by the mere lack of illumination.

Not really so funny.

Right seemed to be the correct direction, so I followed the wall around the corner and walked on.

Solitary footsteps broke the silence again, sounding as if they were somewhere ahead of me.

I raised my voice, louder this time. "Hello? I'm sorry, but I've gotten myself lost. Will you turn on the lights? Please?"

Only maddening, breath-smothering silence.

Moving on, my eyes ached from straining to see.

I'd gone too far. Must have missed my turn.

I pivoted and began my trek back the way I came, sliding my hand along the wall, stumbling across the intersection where I'd made the wrong turn.

In this corridor, I came to a door. A room. There would be a light switch just inside.

I grabbed the handle and turned. Locked. Moving on, faster this time, I found another door and almost cried when the knob wouldn't turn.

Why were the rooms bolted? I told myself to calm down. The workers secured the rooms because construction was still in progress. Rational dissolved in the pitch-black corridor. My heart pounded against my chest, and panic boiled up from my stomach. I yelled. "Help! I'm in the hallway and I'm lost. It's too dark to find my way out."

I paused, took a couple deep breaths, and begged, "It's silly, I know. Please turn on a light for me."

No answer, except faint rubbery footsteps from somewhere behind me.

I didn't bother raising my voice. "Who's there?"

With renewed resolution, I forged ahead, one hand on the wall beside me and one stretched out into the ominous future. I came to another corner and fell into the open space. Which way should I turn?

Footfalls behind me. No time to deliberate. I turned right and kept my hand on the wall, my only sense of stability. I continued stumbling along in the dark, moving as fast as possible, straining to listen for the presence of another. My own breathing came too hard and loud for me to hear anything else.

Wait, there ahead I caught a quick glimmer of light. It flashed and was gone in a second, maybe from a passing car. Possibly through a window?

Yes, there must be a window or a door. I ran blindly toward the light, or the hope of the light, until I slammed into a glass door. I must have made it to the back of the building. I laughed with relief at the sight of distant streetlights.

I fumbled for the keypad and after messing up the security code twice, I finally got it punched in and the latch clicked. Pushing the door open tripped the alarm, loud and welcome. Security would be alerted. I stepped outside, bending at the waist to catch my breath.

The alarm stopped abruptly. What? Was the person following me close enough to disengage the siren?

I ran for the street lights, slipped on wet grass and found myself face down in the dirt. My knees stung, but I pushed myself up and trudged on.

The front of Beaver Creek was illuminated, gloriously. I pushed through the lobby door and was so relieved I giggled uncontrollably. The sight of the activities director brought me to my senses. Helen stood alone in the reception area with her clipboard and pen.

She gazed at me for a moment. "Lauren, what on earth happened to you? Are you all right?"

I looked down at my mud-stained hands and knees. "Um, I slipped on the grass out in the yard on the side of the building."

She tipped her head to the side. "Oh, I see. What were you doing out there?"

"It's crazy. I was in Evelyn's Party Room and went back to Louise's room to get my bag. Somewhere along the way the lights went out. I guess an aide, or orderly, or someone, turned them off. I didn't realize it would be so dark. I got lost in the new wing. It was awful until I finally found an outside door."

Helen gave me a gentle smile and explained. "No, dear, we never turn out the corridor lights. That would be dangerous for the residents."

"That's what I thought, but the lights were definitely out." I reached down and brushed at the dirt smudges on my pants.

Helen shook her head. "Are you sure? Because that's unacceptable. We could be sued. Show me where this happened."

She headed for the new residents wing.

I limped along behind her. "I heard someone in the hallway. Footsteps. I guess they were playing a joke on me because they wouldn't answer when I called."

"None of our people would do such a thing. Besides, everyone is helping in the community center. You know any of our employees would have helped you if they'd known you were in distress. There must be some mistake."

The first hallway was brightly lit. I caught up with Helen and limped ahead. "I know I was in this general area—somewhere." We turned the corner to yet another illuminated hallway.

Helen turned to me. "Which lights were out?"

I pointed at the ceiling lights. "These. All of them." We hurried to the next hallway where all the lightbulbs blazed. "All of these lights were out." I kept walking and peered down the next hall.

Helen caught up with me and placed her hand on my shoulder. Her compassionate eyes and smile were so comforting I almost let down my guard. Then I remembered where I'd seen the well-practiced expression, often used on the dementia patients. "Well, as you see, they're all on now. Let's go back to Louise's room and get you cleaned up. And I'll help you get your handbag."

I stood my ground. "I know I didn't imagine it. It was pitch black."

"Uh-huh." She took my hand and tugged me back down the hall until we were in front of Louise's room. I allowed her to guide me to the big green recliner. Helen stepped into the bathroom, while I sat questioning my sanity.

She came out with a wet cloth and gently wiped my hands and my chin. "You've been working very hard lately. When's the last time you had time off? I know living alone is stressful. The responsibility of a house and all. But everyone needs a vacation from time to time. You tell Rarity you want a week off, and maybe take a break from writing too."

She turned the cloth over and dabbed at the stains on the knees of my pants.

Her overly comforting tone of voice began to grate on my nerves. "I know. Why not stay in a cabin at the lake? I bet you can rent one at a reasonable price. Take a rest, enjoy nature, and don't worry about anything."

Helen flashed a bright, annoying smile. "There." Once finished tending to me, she returned the cloth to the bathroom.

"That's an idea." I grabbed my handbag from Louise's bed and hobbled to the door. I just wanted to go home.

"Thanks so much, Helen. Would you tell Louise I was tired and went home?" I left without waiting for an answer and gingerly walked down the corridor.

Helen called out. "Of course. She'll understand. I bet you're worn out. I meant that about taking a break."

I waved over my shoulder and pushed through the front door, making it to the middle of the parking lot before I thought to scope out my surroundings. It was a well-lit lot, but creepy, dark shadows lined the perimeter. Suspicious shapes appeared under trees and near the building. I clambered into my car. After pushing down the door lock, I turned to make sure the other doors were secure.

I'll have to trade this car in for one with automatic locks.

The Chrysler engine roared to life and I shoved it into gear. Imaginary shadows followed me all the way home.

Chapter Fourteen

A beam of sunlight shot through the narrow opening between the curtains. I shielded my eyes from the glare. I'd tossed all night long, my mind sorting through terrors of the evening before.

Had it been a dream? Skinned palms and knees confirmed it had happened. Sore muscles resisted as I flipped over to go back to sleep.

The clock glowed from the nightstand.

Crap. I'd arranged to meet Clair and Anita for coffee.

It would only take one call to cancel. No. I needed to talk to them. Helen hadn't believed me, but my friends would give me their unbiased opinions.

I crawled out of bed and pulled on a pair of jeans. In the light of day, the adventure sounded crazy, even to me. My injuries would prove at least part of it was real.

I filled Mason's food bowl and scratched his ears before finding my keys on the way out.

I was halfway to the car when Murine popped out of the bushes at the side of her yard. Still jumpy from the night before, I skidded to a stop. When my heart slowed down, I laughed. "I was so distracted I didn't see you. How are you?"

"Wonderful. Isn't it a beautiful day?"

My gaze landed on the large butcher knife in her hand. "Uh-huh."

It took me a minute to notice purple flowers in her other hand. "You're cutting a bouquet. How pretty. Are they lilacs?"

Murine smiled. "Yes, I think they are. They've always grown here, but this will be the first bouquet I've taken into the house. Clive always said they'd drop petals on the floor. He never liked the smell either. Can you imagine not loving such a sweet scent? But he's not here now, so I do what I want." She lifted the bouquet to her nose and smiled.

"He's away? That explains it. I mean I usually see him a few times a week, going to and from work, but haven't in a while."

It explained a few other things, such as the new Murine.

A sweet smile took over her face. "Clive took a vacation. A long one, I think."

"That's nice. Where did he go?"

"He's fishing in Canada. A couple of his old buddies talked him into going."

"I take it you're not into fishing?"

Murine shook her head. "Definitely not. Would you believe he's so far up in the wilderness, they don't have electricity or telephones? Not even cell service." She pulled a couple leaves from the branches she held. "I haven't talked to him since he left."

"The trip sounds exciting, but I agree with you. I don't think I'd want to be cut off from civilization like that. Has he been on one of these trips before?"

"No. First time he's traveled anywhere. I could never convince him to take trips. Funny thing is, now that he's gone, I feel like I'm on vacation."

Murine inclined her head toward me, a sweet smile playing on her lips. "It's so quiet and peaceful. I watch television when I want to. I only cook what I want and haven't even had to clean since Clive left."

"So, this is the first time you've been on your own?"

Murine turned and gazed at her house. "It's the first time, ever. We got married right out of high school."

"Aren't you nervous, being alone in the house?"

She turned back toward me. "Oh no. That 12-guage shotgun of Clive's is sitting right by the door." She winked. "I'm pretty sure I could hit what I aimed at."

I studied the thin woman for a minute before I could decide what to say. "You can shoot a shotgun? They have a kick, don't they? Doesn't it throw you off balance?"

Murine gestured with her hand—the one holding the knife. "Not too bad. You have to know how to handle the recoil. The trick is squaring your shoulders." She adjusted her body to show me. "It's what they call the aggressive fighting stance. And brace the gun against the pectoral muscle, not the shoulder."

I was speechless. I'd lived next to this woman for a year and had no idea who she was.

I searched for conversation. "Um, where in Canada did you say Clive went?"

She giggled. "Silly me. I don't know the name of the place. Don't think it even has an address."

"When will he be back?"

"No telling. He said I'd see him when I see him. That's just like Clive. Never tells me his schedule, but as long as he's having a good time, I don't mind."

Murine returned to the lilac bush and sliced off a few more stems with the knife.

"Nice visiting with you, Murine."

She glanced at me, her answer a mere murmur, "Yes. You too."

I left my neighbor to her flowers, and climbed the steps of my porch. Always thought of her as a little different. This was just one more side of Murine. A side I would never have expected.

Mason met me inside the door and stared up at me.

"Shoot. I was on my way out, wasn't I?"

I did an about face, relocked the door, and resumed my trip to Ava's.

~

I closed my mouth, my eyes darting from Anita to Clair and back again. We were at our usual table at Ava's Java, and I'd spilled the whole story of the chase through Beaver Creek. If I thought my friends would be lavish with their sympathy, I was mistaken.

Anita stirred a packet of sugar into her cup. "Lauren, you must quit reading those true crime novels. Maybe a nice romance. At least before bedtime. I don't know how you sleep at all."

I stared at her and shook my head. "I'm not making this up. I know there was someone in that hallway. I heard the footsteps. It scared me to death. Can't even think about what would have happened if they'd caught up with me."

Clair pulled a nail file from her handbag and smoothed a fingernail. "Think about it, Lauren, maybe the building creaks. You know how older buildings have those strange sounds. From the wind or the air conditioner or something."

Concentrating on my breathing to stay calm. "It wasn't the building. Besides, I was in the new construction, not the old. And there were footsteps."

I ran my fingers through my hair, thinking if Clair and Anita didn't stop doubting me, I might pull out a handful. My hair, not theirs. "And why were the lights out? Just as I got close to a corridor, it would go dark. Helen says the halls are always lit. What happened?"

Anita chirped. "I know. Someone spiked the punch."

I looked at her. "They did not. Besides, I didn't have any punch."

I couldn't believe it. Clair actually had a grin on her face. "I bet it was some aide or maintenance guy playing with you. Probably thought you were cute and got a kick out of scaring the pretty lady. Of course, he knew he'd be in trouble when Helen showed up so turned everything back on before she could catch him."

"It didn't feel like a flirtation. And the door alarm? It was only on for a second and went off."

Anita peered at Clair. "Defective, don't you think? Probably the lights, too."

Clair shrugged and tucked the nail file back into her handbag.

Anita returned her gaze to me. "They'll have to get that fixed."

I wanted to lay my head down on the table and scream into the placemat, but took a deep breath and told myself to be mature.

Anita patted my shoulder. "Really, I can't imagine who would do that to you. I bet it was all a mistake."

I eyed Clair. "Do you really think it was a joke?"

"I'm pretty sure it was someone's idea of humor. I bet they got a good laugh out of hearing you try to explain it to Helen. I agree it wasn't very nice, but it was just a joke. Don't worry about it."

Shifting my eyes to Anita. "And what's your final answer?"

Anita smirked. "Like I said, too many crime novels."

"Humph."

I crossed my arms over my chest and stared out the window for few minutes. "Okay, let's forget about that. I don't want to talk about it anymore. But the thefts at The Rare Curl weren't imaginary. I sure wish we knew who did that."

Clair and Anita swiveled their heads toward me and stared as if I'd lost my mind.

Clair put up both hands. "Lauren, that's over. It was petty theft and probably will never be solved. The police aren't worried about it. Rarity has moved on, you should too."

"Well, somebody should be worrying about it. And another thing, my neighbor…"

Clair's attention had drifted. Her eyes were focused toward the top of my head.

She pointed a well-manicured finger at me. "Have you ever worn short hair? I bet it would be really cute."

I grabbed my ponytail. "Short? No. I like it long so I can pull it back."

Clair directed my attention to the counter where Ava spoke to a customer. "Have you noticed Ava's new style? Makes her look younger, don't you think?"

Anita nodded. "It takes years off her face."

At times my friends could be extremely annoying. I decided to throw out a little test. Did they pay attention to anything I had to say? "Not that I'd blame Murine for shooting her husband with his own shotgun."

I waited, looked from one to the other. No reaction.

Anita shifted her attention to me.

She heard me. Wait, no she didn't.

Anita's head tipped to the side. "I can't see it short, but Lauren would look cute in any hairstyle."

Clair bobbed her head. "You're right. I'd love to see it about this length." She slid her fingers under her chin.

Still inspecting my current hairstyle, Anita narrowed her eyes. "Maybe."

My two friends continued the discussion of my appearance while I looked on.

I took two deep cleansing breaths, exhaling lowly. Then I raised my voice and spoke cheerfully. "Oh, look at the time. Must get home and work on an article due this week. Have to get groceries, too. Lots to do today."

My chair tipped as I slid it out. I caught it with one hand while I swung my handbag across my shoulder with the other. "See you later, girls."

They both seemed a little surprised to see me on my feet, but waved as I left.

~

Leaving my friends to their hairstyle discussion, I had other questions whirling through my brain on the drive home. Was it a combination of malfunctions that caused the incident at Beaver Creek? Did my imagination cause it to seem worse than it was? Should I stop reading crime books? I don't like romance novels.

While stopped at a traffic light, I wondered about the thefts at The Rare Curl. Had Rarity moved past it? But she'd said she depended on me to solve the mystery.

I pulled into my driveway wondering how I got there. That was fast. I needed to keep my mind on reality. If they found me dead someday, it probably wouldn't be an Evelynton murder. It would be my silly curiosity and over active imagination.

Chapter Fifteen

I climbed the concrete steps of the hundred-and-fifty-year-old stone building that housed The Evelynton Times newspaper office. The post office had been there when I graduated from high school. Sometime in the years since, the postal service upgraded to a modern structure. I guess the newspaper didn't mind creaking floors or leaky windows.

Couldn't help but be proud of myself for finishing an article that might make a difference to the elderly residents of the nursing home. I would have been prouder to be able to hand the editor a printed copy, but Donald Daily's desk was covered with stacks of paper. My work might be lost for weeks.

A young reporter sat at wooden desk near the door, engrossed in her work. I marched to the editor's office and tapped on the door.

"Who is it now?" I'd become accustomed to Daily's gruff manor. Always sounded as if he was about to bite. I pushed the door open a crack and peeked in. He was just visible between the stacks of newspapers and books piled on his desk. A layer of dust coated the books, the visible edges of the desk, and his computer monitor.

"Come in, Lauren. How have you been? Catch any more criminals lately? Hey, I heard you were on the scene and found the unidentified body. Why didn't you give me a call?"

"I didn't find it."

Donald wasn't listening. "We can still use it. Talk to Tracy on the way out."

"Clair Lane actually did the discovering. You should have Tracy talk to her. I'm here to tell you about the Beaver Creek Rehab Center article."

"Why do you waste your time with those fluff stories? I'd jump on an up-close-and-personal testimony of finding the body in the gully."

He flashed a grin. "Maybe call it 'Death in the Ravine.'"

"Thanks, Donald. But I didn't see it up close. Made an effort not to see it all. And I really don't have the desire to write that kind of news. Thought I did once, when I didn't realize what it entailed. With that murder last year and a few other incidents, I've lost my desire to write about crime. I may even quit reading about it."

"I don't believe that for a second. It's in your blood. You're a local hero. You cracked that other case wide open."

How many times had I gone through that with Donald Daily? "I'm not a hero. All I did was interrupt a thief in my house. Didn't tackle her. Didn't even suspect Patsy Clooney of the thefts, let alone the murder. In fact, I'd pegged someone else entirely."

"Ha, ha. Okay. Humility is a good thing. You prefer to keep a low profile, but we know better." He winked at me and shuffled some papers on his desk.

"Anyway, Donald, I finished the article on the residents of Beaver Creek. It should be in your inbox." I felt I needed to remind Donald to check his email. Afraid his account was as stacked as his desk.

The editor focused his attention on the computer and tapped the keyboard. The monitor sprang to life.

Gratified the machine was turned on, I continued. "I titled it 'Halls of Wisdom,' but I'm open if you come up with something better."

"The lonely old people article, right?"

"Yes. But we won't call it that, will we?"

Donald shrugged.

"This article will be good for the nursing home and for the town. The Beaver Creek residents are great people, and if given a chance, they'll capture hearts. We have good citizens in this town who are unaware of the need. I know there will be more visitors after this is published."

"You think so? You have more faith in people than I have." Donald grabbed a stack of papers and blew at the cloud of dust it released.

"Helen, the activities director, and I put together a program called Extended Family. I outlined it in the article. People call in, and Helen gives them the name and birthday of a resident with no close family of their own. The citizens commit to two days a month, one day every other week, to visit their resident. They'll stay at least half an hour. It can be as easy as sitting with their resident during game time or when outside entertainment comes in. They also commit to sending birthday cards, Christmas cards, etc. That's the starter program. After that, they can go as far as planning birthday parties and buying small gifts."

It seemed to me the editor's eyes were glazing over. "You aren't listening, are you? Do you want to wait and read the article?"

He gave his head a quick shake, possibly to wake himself up. "No, no. I'm listening, Go ahead."

"Okay. This will be great for the town. We're expecting enough of a response that each resident will have more than one Extended Family member. Several can even work together if they want. They can plan visits on different days so the resident is occupied more often. They can work together in planning a birthday party. The nursing home has Santa visit during the Christmas season, so the citizens can have their picture taken with Santa and their adopted resident."

"Ha. How do you know the people will keep up their side of the bargain?"

"Most of them will. I'm sure there will be times when people are too busy and may miss a day. And some who decide it's more work than they expected and will quit. Helen will keep the records. They sign in at each visit. That way Helen will know if a resident is left without an Extended Family. Some will love it and maybe have two or even three residents to visit. If needed, they could plan little parties with several residents together."

"People are too busy." Donald restacked a pile of papers on his desk. I took it as a signal he was finished with the conversation.

"I guess we'll see, Donald. Remember to look for the attachment in your inbox."

He'd probably be more interested in a story of my terrifying chase through the dark halls of the nursing home, but I no longer wanted to talk about that.

Chapter Sixteen

Despite the discouraging newspaper man, I climbed into my car with a smile on my face. I'd finished the newspaper article. A project that had been different from anything I'd accomplished before. It sounded like a day to celebrate by watching an old movie, or maybe with a nap.

A starving writer's wishful thinking. The bills wouldn't pay themselves unless I wrote more articles.

I pulled into traffic. At least I'd enjoy the scenery on the drive home.

People were out strolling and enjoying the sunshine. Patricia Martin was running a sale on sundresses.

There was a surprise. Murine Baron stood in front of the dress shop, gazing at the new display. Never thought of her as a window shopper. I wondered if she would go in and come out with a new dress. I bet it wouldn't be gray.

My guess was Clive hadn't returned from his fishing trip.

Enjoy your freedom, Murine.

At home, I dreaded jumping into another writing project. A little more time was needed. I picked up Mason and cuddled the purring cat while I wandered to the back porch.

"Talk to me, Mason. Is the town getting stranger? Is my imagination getting out of control?" Murine had definitely changed. "What do you think has happened to our neighbor, furry friend?"

I opened the screen door and carried the cat down the steps to the yard. After I'd put him on the ground, I walked to the side of my property. If my life was a romance novel, I'd say the birds and flowers drew me there. In truth, I wanted to check out the Barons' backyard while no one was at home.

The property was empty. A plain yard. Nothing to attract my attention. What was I expecting? Evidence of the digging of a fresh grave? Maybe traces of the alien spaceship that had abducted Murine and replaced her with a strong happy, woman?

Mason's whiskers tickled my ankles and I glanced down at him. "Do you suppose aliens abducted Clive?"

All the windows of the house were open, curtains fluttering in the breeze. I could almost imagine it breathing. Looked like the place was taking deep gulps of fresh air. Just like Murine. She seemed to have come alive and was breathing for the first time.

Still, why would Clive, who never went anywhere except work, take a vacation without her?

My eyes focused on the Barons' back door. Was it locked? She'd left the windows open, maybe the door was unlatched.

I pushed branches away from my face as I stepped through the bushes, into my neighbor's yard.

The solid door stood open, only the screen door was closed. Was I brave enough to test it?

Anita was right. I'd been reading far too many true crime novels. Still, I couldn't help myself. I crept closer.

A man's voice sounded as if it was right behind me. "Lauren."

I jumped and tripped over Mason as I spun around. Peering through the shrubs, I saw Wallace, not behind me, but standing at my back door. His attention was focused on my porch. He hadn't discovered me trespassing on the Barons' property.

Casually, and as quietly as possible, I pushed through the hedge and stepped into my own yard. "Hi, Wallace. I'm over here."

Wallace whirled around. "I didn't even see you there. Must be getting' old and losing my touch."

"Just checking out my shrubs. Um, wondering if I need to trim them." What kind of story was that? I'd never trimmed a bush in my life. One look at my yard made it painfully obvious that I knew nothing about lawn care. "It's good to see you. How've you been?"

Wallace jumped down from the steps and strode toward me. "What's going on around here? Just talked to Rarity. I was out of town for a few weeks and found out somebody stole from her beauty shop. Then you unearthed a corpse. That was quite a discovery."

"The body was not my discovery. I never even saw it clearly. It was Clair. Unfortunately, she got the close-up view."

Wallace stood with his hands in his pockets. "You feel alright staying in the house alone?"

"Sure. This neighborhood has been peaceful. I always feel safe here."

My thoughts flew to Clive. "Since you're here, there is something I want to talk to you about. Just something that doesn't seem right. You know the Barons'." I motioned to their house. "Did you know Clive went…"

Wallace whirled to look toward his house and the sound of a car pulling into the drive. "Sounds like that's at my house. Guess I've got company. Better go."

He angled through my yard, trotting toward his driveway.

"Bye Wallace."

Silly thought anyway.

With a last glance at the Barons', I started back to my porch.

The sound of manly voices from Wallace's drive piqued my curiosity. I detoured to check out the perennials, or weeds, between my house and Wallace's. A stealthy glance revealed an older model, tan Chevy sedan in his drive. Beside it stood Wallace's old friend, Jack Spencer.

I bent over as if to pull a weed and studied the two from the corner of my eye. Jack was easily as handsome as the last time I saw him over a year ago. But what happened to his fine ride? The tan Chevy didn't hold a candle to the slick, black SUV he'd driven as an FBI agent.

My concentrated effort to listen revealed only bits of conversation. Nothing that made sense.

The two men walked to Wallace's front door. It's slamming was the last I heard from them.

I stared at the little flower garden—or weed patch—trying to act as if I had a purpose for being there. Before long I began to feel awkward. I couldn't kill time any longer.

Mason sat at my feet and purred. I whispered, "I know you think I've lost my mind." No better option presented itself, so I pulled the cat into my arms and carried him into the house. He promptly jumped to the floor to inspect his food dish.

When in doubt, clean house. I kept myself occupied for an hour by moving clutter from one table to another, interspersed with frequent glances through the window toward Wallace's drive.

Bored and tired of waiting, I stretched out on the sofa to read a magazine. Male voices filtering in from outside sent me rolling to the floor. Jack and Wallace had finally emerged. I scrambled to my feet and to the front door.

In my excitement, more force was applied to the handle than necessary. The door flew open throwing me off balance. I regained my composure, and kept my eyes focused on the potted plant on the porch. Me—a concerned gardener, picking off leaves and blossoms.

I may have destroyed the plant.

A car door slammed, and I raised my head just in time to see the Chevy back out of Wallace's drive. Before I could make my feet move, Jack was traveling down Stonybridge Drive.

I kicked the flower pot.

Geesh. Couldn't I have walked over to say hello? I might have waved to get his attention. Too late. The opportunity had dissolved as the Chevy drove out of sight.

Chapter Seventeen

Thanks Gladys." I cashed out Rarity's customer, my last duty for the day at the salon.

As soon as Gladys left, Rarity sidled up beside me. "I'll walk out with you. Didn't bring my lunch today, so I'll pick up a sandwich at Ava's Java and bring it back to the salon to eat while Paula's color is processing."

The two of us walked to the entrance where I pushed open the door to allow the older woman to go ahead of me.

"Coming through." The shout came from a passing mobility scooter. I pulled the door back a few inches to allow Deloris D'agostino extra leeway as she motored down the sidewalk.

"Oops. Almost had a collision." Rarity laughed. "Isn't it nice those motorized chairs allow people such freedom? Not long ago that woman would have had to depend on someone to push her in a wheelchair."

Ava's Java was only two doors down from The Rare Curl, but we had to navigate through a crowded sidewalk. While we chatted, Rarity collided with a pretty teen with long, shiny black hair. Rarity apologized. "Excuse me. I was talking and not paying attention."

The girl tore her attention away from her cell phone and looked at us with startled green eyes. "Oh, I'm so sorry. It was probably my fault. I know I'm not supposed to text while I walk."

"Don't worry, dear. No harm done." Rarity tipped her head for a closer look at the girl's face. "It's Melody, isn't it? Do you remember me, Rarity Peabody?"

"Sure, you're from the hair salon. It was so nice of you to talk to me the other day. I learned a lot about the beauty business."

"I hope I was helpful. I remember I was busy with a customer at the time and didn't have much time to show you around."

"You supplied what I needed. I can't wait to go to cosmetology school. As soon as I finish, I'll be back to see you. Sure hope I can work for you."

"I'll do my best to find a job for you. You seem like an enterprising young woman."

Rarity put her hand on my arm. "This is Lauren Halloren, our receptionist."

Rarity twisted toward me. "Melody visited the salon, exploring the hairdressing business."

"Hi Melody. I think I've met you before. Maybe at Ava's?"

"Yes. I work there part time. I pass the salon on my way to work. When I look in the window, it seems like you all have so much fun."

Melody shot a glance toward the street. "There's my ride. I have to run. You have a good day, Mrs.

Peabody. It was nice to meet you, Mrs. Halloren." She waited for traffic to clear, jogged across the street and climbed into a navy sedan with tinted windows. I hated windows that prevented a view of the inside. Not because I'm nosy. I have a curious nature.

I turned my attention back to Rarity and hurried to catch up. She had stepped into Ava's Java.

Rarity stood in front of me in line at the counter. "You know, Lauren, Melody is an impressive young woman. She saw my ad for a hairdresser and stopped in to find out all she could about the salon industry. The girl was fascinated with all the ins and outs of the business, even how we make appointments. Melody has the makings of a fine hairdresser. Polite, nice personality, and assertive."

"It's good to see a young person planning for the future. When did she visit The Rare Curl? Must have been on my day off."

We stepped steadily forward toward the counter as each customer ahead received their order. "Oh, I guess it's been a few weeks. I was kind of busy at the time, but we talked, and I told her to take a look around. I recommended the best cosmetology schools in the area. A successful career begins with a good education."

At that, Rarity examined the menu on the wall. While she decided, I scanned the tables, looking for Clair or Anita.

Wait. I was there on the wrong day. Shoot.

"Geesh, Rarity, I forgot I was going straight home today. I don't meet Clair and Anita until tomorrow. Got my days mixed up."

I stepped out of line and took two steps toward the door before I began to rethink my decision. Ava's Java had good lunches. "Maybe a sandwich to go." I stepped back into line behind Rarity.

"No, I'm not that hungry. I can find something at home." This time I half swiveled toward the door, but didn't get out of line. Hate these decisions.

I performed that little dance one more time. The woman in line behind me glared. "Sorry, I'm going to stay after all." She didn't say a word. I thought she was very patient.

Rarity ordered a grilled ham and cheese to go.

Ava gave the order to the cook and returned. "And what can I get for you, Lauren?"

"I'll have the same with coffee. For here. I'll be staying."

Rarity and I moved aside to wait for our food. "So you have placed an ad for another hairdresser. Stacy will be pleased."

"It's time. I know I let it go too long, but I think we all had to get over last year's trauma. Stacy's been a trouper. I know she prefers to work at a slower pace, not the tight schedule we've been on for the last year."

Ava's voice drew our attention back to the counter. "Here you go, ladies. All set. One to go, and one with coffee to stay."

I bid good-bye to Rarity again and took my tray to a table near the window. Not my favorite seat—someone else had claimed it—but one that provided a clear view of the busy street outside.

I'd settled in and pulled out my notebook and pen, when the atmosphere took a turn. A shadow materialized over my table.

"Good afternoon, Ms. Halloren." The words sent tingles up my spine. I lifted my head to see the man whose deep voice I couldn't forget. A teasing smile played at his eyes.

I dropped the pen. "Agent Spencer, um Jack, this is a surprise."

I wish I wrote romance, so I could come up with a reply that was lyrical and enticing. I couldn't be more boring if I was doing the farm report.

After an awkward two seconds of silence, with me staring into his eyes, he asked, "May I sit?"

"Of course. Please do."

My impressive word skills probably had him stunned.

I sorted through my storehouse of snappy conversation topics. Came up with only "In town again, I see."

Jack smiled or maybe almost laughed. "I stopped in to see Wallace Binion, but he wasn't home. Guess I should have called first. I'm hoping he'll be back before I have to return to Indianapolis. I'm working from there now."

Should I let him go on or admit Clair already told me?

"Yes. I knew that. Clair Lane said she spoke to you."

No! Now he knew we talked about him.

My wandering thoughts caused another pause in the conversation. I clasped my cup and took a sip.

"Clair mentioned you have a new business venture. Security consultant? What does that involve?"

No! Now he knew we actually had a discussion about him.

Jack took a few minutes to describe his company. Sadly, I don't remember a word of it. Light from the window reflected in his dark eyes. One strand of hair strayed onto his forehead. I hadn't noticed the silver streaks at his temples. They were in the perfect place. Why do men look great with gray hair?

He'd stopped talking.

Shoot. Was it my turn to talk? Should I ask him why he left the FBI? *No.* That would be prying. Or maybe he already told me.

"Umm. Will you miss the Florida beaches?"

Lame. Really lame.

He raised his eyebrows. "I haven't had time to think about it, yet. Probably not."

Lines formed on his forehead. "I've wanted to talk to you, to apologize for the misunderstanding about your late husband. I know it's an emotional subject for you, and I won't go into it again, except to say how sorry I am to have caused you pain."

My thoughts flashed back to the scene a year ago, when he'd suggested my late husband had been involved in drug activity. I'd freaked out.

Forcing myself back to the conversation, "It's fine, really. You already apologized when you called to let me know you'd closed the case. No need for more apologies. Let's put it behind us."

Jack blew out a breath. Had he been holding his breath? "Splendid idea. Let's change the subject. What shall we talk about?"

I didn't care what we talked about. I just wanted to listen to his voice.

When I didn't respond, he went on. "I remember you're a writer. Tell my about your work."

This wasn't something I liked to talk about. I could have said I'd authored a book. A bestseller—except I hadn't. Instead I found myself telling former FBI Agent Jack Spencer all about my fluffy articles, designed for old people. He listened to my boring chatter. His eyes didn't stray from mine. And, bless him, he didn't yawn.

Then I told him of my long-time wish to write a true crime novel. I even told him about discovering I had no understanding of crime or criminals. He still refrained from displaying signs of boredom, so I admitted my blunders in last year's murder case— things I hadn't shared with anyone.

I couldn't stop talking, and moved on to Rarity's missing hair color. Fortunately, I regained my sanity and slammed on the brakes just short of confessing to the stakeout at The Rare Curl. The man would be sure I was a lunatic.

The ice had broken and he related a few stories of his career. We laughed. We got quiet, but it was comfortable. It was that special silence between two people beginning to like one another.

Our eyes met and lingered. I told my heart to stop fluttering.

A noise threatened to pull me away from that warm place. I struggled to concentrate as my mind registered the clickety-clack approach of high-heels. Clair Lane's high heels. I would have known that sound anywhere.

She shrieked. "Lauren. Hey girl, I didn't know you would be here to..."

I glanced up to greet her. Too late. She stood at my side with eyes fixed and dilated on Jack Spencer.

Clair recovered quickly. "Oh, my goodness. Jack. I am so happy to see you."

She leaned forward with one hand on our table, facing him. This left me with a clear view of the back of her head. I shifted to the left, far enough to imagine I was still part of the conversation.

Clair's voice was melodic and interesting. "Jack, I wanted to tell you how much I appreciated our talk. I know we only had a few minutes when I caught up with you in Indianapolis, but those few words worked wonders. You gave me such peace about that horrific experience of finding the dead person." Clair shuddered, then gave her shoulders a feminine shrug. "I'm so grateful. Can't believe my luck finding you here. No, I know better. It wasn't luck at all. It was kismet. Destiny."

I leaned a bit further to the left in hopes of rejoining the team. Jack stared at Clair, wide-eyed and mute.

Clair didn't seem to register his "deer in headlights" expression. "Jack, I've wanted to repay your kindness. No, I need to repay you." The woman spoke as though they were the only two in the room. She straightened and checked the time. She groaned, in a very feminine way. "Darn, I have a client meeting in ten minutes. Just came in for a cup."

Yes! She had to leave.

Clair, focused as she was on Jack, seemed to have forgotten I was there. "Where will you be later this afternoon? I must buy you dinner. There's a charming little diner at the edge of town. Very quiet, where we can talk. I know you'll love it. Let's see, I can meet you at...."

As Clair paused for a breath, Jack blurted out an answer. "That's nice of you, but not at all necessary." He lifted his left hand to indicate his watch. "In fact, I have an appointment right now. And after that, unfortunately I'm due at the office. Back in the city. Important clients."

Clair shook her head. Amazingly, she was still able to display her newly whitened teeth. "I won't take no for an answer, handsome. I'm so indebted to you."

Jack scooted his chair out and stood. "I appreciate the gesture. I really do. Maybe some other time. Just realized I'm already late for that appointment."

He caught my gaze while he pushed his chair in. "Nice seeing you, Lauren."

He nodded at Clair. "Good to see you, too. Um, we'll be in touch."

The man exited as if being chased. Strange to see a former FBI agent in full-panic mode.

Clair gazed after him. "He's so attractive. That must have been an important appointment. Maybe I should have walked out with him. What do you think?"

I shook my head. "Nooo. It sounded like he was in a big hurry."

She let out a sigh and gazed through the window. "Darn, I wish I'd known he was in town. I'd have worn my red dress."

Clair put her hands on her hips and glanced at me. "Oh well, there will be another time. Better get to my own meeting. Anita and I will see you here tomorrow for lunch. Right?"

With my assurance that I'd be there, she grabbed her to-go cup and trotted to the door.

I sat there wondering at the last half hour.

Did I almost have a romantic moment with Jack Spencer? Was it my imagination?

Silly me. What was I thinking? Dating Jack Spencer? Not likely. He said he'd be in touch with Clair.

Even if I'd had a chance with him, I wouldn't want to cut in. Clair was clearly smitten with him. Friends were too important.

I'd lost my appetite. After I packed up my notebook and pen, I dropped my dish at the counter and headed home, where I should have gone in the first place.

Chapter Eighteen

The front door of The Rare Curl slammed open, sending the string of bells flying. Stacy stalked in with clenched fists and a scowl that could sour milk.

"Good morning, Stacy. Having a rough morning?"

She stopped for an instant beside the desk. "I don't believe it. Judy's hair is black." She continued to her styling chair.

There were many times I struggled to understand Stacy's thoughts, but this really had me wondering. "How is that a problem? And who is Judy?"

Stacy raised her voice. "I just saw my customer, Judy Winters, at the drug store. She'd tinted her hair herself. At least I think she did it herself. I sure hope she didn't pay for that. It looked awful."

"Did you ask her about it? What did she say?"

Stacy whipped her face in my direction and looked at me as if I'd sprouted horns. "Of course not. I pretended I didn't notice." She returned to pulling combs and brushes from the drawer and throwing them on her station. "I can't believe it. I've been doing her hair for years. She was always happy. Never once told me she wanted something different. Then she goes and does that—whatever she's done."

Stacy straightened and shook her finger at her own reflection in the mirror. "I should've known. A few weeks ago, she asked what I used on her." Plopping into her chair, she shook her head. "Didn't think anything of it at the time."

Part of my job description was calming hysterical stylists. I scrolled through my mental file of Rarity's reassuring remarks. "You don't know what's been in Judy's mind, or what's been going on in her life. Don't let it get you down. Just think about all the women who love your work." Proud of my insightful response, I lifted the appointment book. "Have you seen your schedule today? It's full."

Stacy's shoulders dropped a little, and she relaxed her hands. "You're right, Lauren. Thanks for the encouragement."

She leaned back, visibly relaxed. Then she took a deep breath and let it out while she performed little waving motions with her hands. They fluttered from the top of her head to her waistline and back up. I thought I'd misjudged my effect on her. Maybe she was having a mental episode.

Then Stacy chanted. "Negativity, go away. Positive, come in. Negative thoughts, go away."

Rarity walked out of the supply room at that moment. She stopped and stared at Stacy. "What are you doing?"

Stacy maintained her exercise. "I'm breathing out negativity. There was a guy on television teaching how to have a happy life. He said when you get mad at someone, to just shoo bad thoughts away. He was wonderful."

Rarity continued to her own styling station and pulled open a drawer. "Really? When I find myself in a bad mood, I give those thoughts to the Lord. He shows me that my feelings don't have to be dictated by someone else's actions. Sometimes I'm not viewing the situation clearly, or I'm taking it personally when it isn't about me at all. Most importantly, I ask him to help me forgive the person."

"I should ask God to help me forgive Judy? No way."

Rarity raised her eyebrows.

"Well, maybe I'll try it." Stacy began pulling out equipment from her styling station to get ready for her first customer.

Rarity unfolded a shampoo cape and draped it over the back of her chair. "Let's go to lunch sometime this week and talk about it."

Stacy smiled. "Okay. I'd like that."

Out of the corner of my eye, I noticed she quietly did a few more hand waves while she finished setting up.

The day had begun with typical weirdness, but I was learning to go with the flow in Evelynton, Indiana. "I think I'll brew a pot of coffee while the phone is quiet."

The next few hours progressed without incident.

~

I hung up the desk phone. "Stacy, you'll never believe this."

She looked up from her magazine. "I'll believe anything. What is it?"

"That was Judy Winters calling for a haircut appointment. I scheduled her with you tomorrow afternoon."

Stacy slapped the magazine shut. "Just a haircut? Not color correction?"

"Haircut and style. This is your chance to ask her about it. As her hairdresser, you have a right to know what's going on with her color."

Stacy sneered and shook the magazine at me. "I should tell her she needs to shave it off and start over."

Pulling out more of Rarity's encouraging remarks. "I've worked here long enough to know you can fix anything. You know you can improve the shade."

"Sure I can fix it. But I'd rather scare her first. If she experienced a little panic, she'd never do it again."

I was on a roll. "Think about it. This is only one incident in a long career as your customer. You want to keep her business, don't you? You'll get further by being nice."

Stacy let out a deep sigh. "Okay. I'll keep calm. I'll have to banish negative thoughts all morning."

She began the hand fluttering again. I wondered where the younger generation got those ideas. And then I wondered how I got to be the older generation? I was only forty-four.

The clock on my desk read twelve noon. The previous four hours felt like a full day's work. I pulled the strap of my handbag over my shoulder. "I'm finished today, ladies. Have a good day."

At the door, I spun around. "And Stacy. If Judy really did her own color, ask her where she got it."

Stacy had moved into my chair at the desk. "She'll probably say she picked it up at the drugstore."

"Maybe so, but I'd like to know for sure. The Rare Curl's disappearing hair color is still a mystery."

Looking forward to lunch, I hurried to Ava's Java where I would meet Clair and Anita. The heavenly aroma of fresh-ground coffee beans met me at the door. I inhaled deeply. Loved the taste of coffee, but I might be able to live on the aroma.

I approached the counter. "Hi, Ava. I'll have a bowl of your tomato bisque and a cup of coffee."

"Sure thing. Your friends are in the other corner today. It was the only table available."

While Ava stepped away to fill my lunch order, I caught Anita's eye and waved. Anita waved back and pointed to the remaining chair at the table.

I gripped my tray to keep it level and weaved my way through the crowded coffee shop.

"Hey, girls. What's up today?

Anita put down her spoon. "Clair's making a life change."

I turned my gaze to Clair and waited to hear her newest adventure.

She leaned back in her chair. "I've decided to buy a house. Maybe get a dog. Apartment living doesn't give me enough space to enjoy my home. And I'm tired of being so needy. No more waiting for the right man to come into my life."

I took a swig of my coffee, thinking of Rarity's words on forgiveness. "What caused this change of heart? Wasn't it yesterday you'd found your perfect man?"

"Oh, you mean Jack Spencer. I've changed my mind. When I thought about it, he acted sort of strange.

Do you remember how he was in such a hurry to leave? He seemed disinterested. Did you notice that, Lauren?"

I shrugged. "I'm not sure I know what you mean." I try my best to be honest, but wasn't about to tell her I thought Jack left as if being chased by cannibals.

Clair continued. "Anyway, I happened to pass him in my car yesterday afternoon. He was on Main Street and I didn't recognize him at first. Did you know he's driving an old Chevy? And it's beige. I saw him in a whole new light."

Anita slurped her soup and replaced the spoon. "Clair, you're not basing love on the kind of car a man drives, are you?"

Clair paused for a moment before she answered. "Of course not. But I realized I'd fallen in love with the image, not the man. I don't even know him. I was enamored with a perception. An FBI agent who drove a cool SUV. He's not with the FBI anymore, and that car…. I want someone who's dependable."

Anita nodded. "That's very wise of you."

"At forty-four, it's time. Stability, not flash."

Clair pointed an index finger at me. I was struck by how bright her red nail polish was. "Like Lauren. She has a house and a yard. And a cat. That's the life. I'm getting a house and maybe a dog. If a man fits in, so be it. If not, that's okay."

Me? She envied my life? Someone had definitely put drugs in Evelynton's water supply.

On the upside, maybe this meant she no longer had her heart set on Jack Spencer.

Life was good.

~

The following morning, I rose early, got some

work done and set off for the salon. I'd waited until I thought Stacy had finished with Judy Winters. Hoping not to be the instigator of another Stacy meltdown in front of too many customers, I peered through the window of The Rare Curl. Rarity had one customer, but Stacy was free. Not many witnesses. I'd keep the conversation simple and uplifting.

"Stacy, I happened to be in town and wondered how your talk with Judy went. She was in this morning, wasn't she?"

Stacy stopped sweeping and rolled her eyes. "Her appointment went alright. Close up, her hair was even worse than I thought. It looked like a Halloween wig. I talked her into a shorter haircut to get rid of the mushy, fried ends. I took your advice and kept what I my thoughts to myself."

Rarity looked up from shampooing her customer. "I was proud of Stacy. She handled it like a pro."

"That's great. I knew you would." Truthfully, I didn't know she would, so much as hoped she would. She might easily have thrown the woman out of the shop or gone after her with the clippers.

I pressed on. "I wonder, did you discover where Judy got the color?"

"She said her cousin ordered hair tint off the Internet and sent it to her. Judy was so pleased because it was supposed to be professional grade."

Stacy stored the broom and planted her hands on her hips. "She said it was the same brand I use. I let her know—nicely—that it was impossible. Our supply house sells only to professionals and no professional would sell it on the Internet."

The hairdresser's voice steadily rose in pitch as she

continued her story. "Then Judy said, 'Oh no, you can get anything on the Internet.' Maybe she's right, I don't know. Anyways, they found it on some auction site."

Stacy might have been on stage, the way she waved her hands while pacing from the reception area to her styling station. "Just goes to show you, it isn't the brand, it's the artist. Judy didn't know any better than to plaster it on all over, so the ends turned that weird color. Believe me, I won't be giving her any hints as to what she's doing wrong. This is my livelihood. I'll wait till she wakes up one day to the mess she's made."

The wise person in me whispered, *Change the subject, Lauren.* But that other, curious person said aloud, "I wonder what Internet site the cousin got it from? Do you think she would still have the return address?"

Stacy stopped and stared at me for a moment. I thought she might explode, but she shrugged. "I don't know. I think the cousin lives in Ohio. The product was probably fake, from China, or something."

Across the room, Rarity's customer raised her head, splattering water down the sides of the shampoo bowl. "Did you say somebody tinted her own hair? With hair color from China? I wouldn't dare."

Rarity murmured, "Oops. Let's put your head back into the bowl, dear." She grabbed a towel to mop up water that had sprayed down the back of the chair and onto the floor.

The wise person in me persisted. *Time to change the subject.* That other ornery person inside me refused.

I lowered my voice, hoping Rarity and her customer wouldn't hear. "Stacy, would you mind calling Judy and asking?"

Stacy glared at me, and I took a step back. Thankfully, she kept her voice at a reduced volume. "Why would I do that? I don't even want to talk about it."

"Just to help solve the mystery here at The Rare Curl. You could keep the conversation light. Simply ask about the website or the return address on the package." I had little hope Stacy would keep that conversation light, when she took it personally.

Was Rarity listening? What would she say if the salon lost the woman's business?

Stacy grunted and turned to her styling station without another word. I almost repeated the query in hopes of an affirmative response, but the wise person in me won out. Instead, I wished everyone a good day and went home.

~

Later that evening, the phone interrupted my TV time.

Stacy began without introduction. "I hope you appreciate this. I phoned Judy Winters and she called her cousin. Then I had to call Judy again because she didn't get back to me. The cousin found the package in the garbage. It was shipped from, get this, Harold, Indiana. That's only in the next county, isn't it? Who would have thought? The name was DMC Enterprises, with only a post office box as the address."

"Great information. Would you call her back? I want the package and the empty bottle for proof."

"Oh, that's not going to happen. She pulled it out of the garbage for the address and told me she put it back in the can just before the truck got there."

That was disappointing.

I wrote down the information Stacy had given me, and later searched the Internet until my seat hurt. I discovered nothing. There was no company named DMC Enterprises listed. But I had faith the Internet held answers to all questions, so I searched for the P.O Box. I was wrong, of course. Sometimes you have to talk to real people.

Chapter Nineteen

Anita sprawled on my sofa, arm draped over the side, while she trailed a string for Mason to play with. She'd been listening to my recap of the previous day's events.

I finished my review and looked to Anita for comment. Her eyes sparkled and a grin took over her face. Something was up. She swung her feet to the floor. "Road trip!"

"What? Where?"

"Let's drive to Harold. I bet you one of Ava's Tall Mochas I can find out who owns that post office box."

"Really? How would you do that? Just ask? Somehow I doubt post office employees are allowed to give out information like that." I thought about it for a moment. "They're not, are they?"

Anita fixed innocent eyes on me. "I suppose not, but you know how small-town folks are. We love to talk. Harold's tiny, and I doubt if anything exciting happens there. They'll talk to anyone who happens by, just for the conversation."

Anita saw the question still reflected in my expression. "I guess you've forgotten how to be a small-town woman. Don't worry. I have faith the Evelynton consciousness will come back to you."

She was right. In the twenty-five years I'd been away, I'd lost my small-town identity. I was stuck in the world where friends communicated by text, and strangers never talked to one another. Except for an occasional 'excuse me,' or something not so courteous, when you cut them off in traffic.

I didn't have confidence the drive would produce anything worthwhile. Then again, it would be a drive in the country. What else did I have to do? "Okay. We might as well go. I doubt we'll discover anything helpful, but it's a nice day for a road trip."

Anita looked into my eyes. "I know you don't believe me, but listen to this. I knew when Patricia Martin at the dress shop was going to have a sale on those gingham shirts my girls wear, 'cause Francis at the post office told me a big shipment came in."

"Uh-huh."

"Now, follow me here. The shipment didn't even go through the post office, but Georgeanne, the mail carrier, happened to be in the store when the truck unloaded at the dress shop. Then Julie, the sales clerk, told Georgeanne they would be putting the old stock on sale. And Georgeanne told Francis at the post office. See how it works?"

"I lost you somewhere in there, but I see your point. Word travels in a small town. Still, a sale on gingham shirts isn't confidential information."

"No, but once Francis gets talking, she spills everything. You know how boring a job like that can be on a slow day. She's usually dying for someone to talk to. I'm sure the people in Harold are no different."

Anita bounced up off the sofa, startling the cat in the middle of his bath. He took off to hide under the side chair. "I love this sleuthing stuff. Never even thought of investigating a crime before you came home. Let's go."

Was I a bad influence on Anita? First, the midnight stakeout. Now this. How would Jake feel about his wife becoming an amateur detective.

"Okay, let me get my handbag. I need to find out who took Rarity's supplies. I just hope I'm as lucky at obtaining information as you are."

Anita put her hand on my shoulder and gave me a serious stare. "Oh, no. I'll do the talking. I have that small-town look. Everybody trusts me." She smiled sweetly. "You are beautiful and look innocent too, but you're a big-city kind of girl. We have to stick to our strengths."

Somehow I didn't connect no makeup and hair in a ponytail with the city, but Anita was fairly perceptive in judging personalities.

"Are you sure you want to do this? I keep worrying about legality."

"You know I won't lie, and I won't pry—too much. I'll simply be myself. We'll see what the clerk tells me. Can't be arrested for listening. Can I?"

Mason had ventured out of hiding, ears flattened and tail thrashing. Anita stepped over him and stood by the door. "We're wasting time."

No time to worry about the kind of influence I'd had on my friend. I wanted the information, and Anita was jingling her keys.

~

I'd described Evelynton as a small town, but it was a metropolis compared to Harold. The tiny town sported little more than one main street, a few mom-and-pop businesses, and the post office.

All parking spaces were vacant, so we pulled into a prime location at the front entrance. We climbed the concrete steps, and I pulled open the heavy door allowing Anita to enter first. On our right was a small bank of safety deposit boxes. On the left, a woman stood behind a wide counter. She brightened as we walked in.

"Good afternoon. How can I help you? Do you need directions?" I guess she knew every Harold resident.

Anita moseyed up to the counter and gushed to the clerk, saying something about the lovely architecture of the building and the beautiful day. I didn't trust myself to keep a straight face, so I feigned interest in a display of collector stamps.

Within a few minutes, giggles bubbled from the area of the counter. Anita and the woman had their heads together as if they were long-lost buddies. I was pretty sure the clerk was spilling everything she knew. Just hoped she knew who owned P.O.Box 101.

Anita glanced at the clock. "Would you look at that? Beth, it's so much fun talking to you, I lost track of time. Thanks for the chat."

"Have a nice day, Anita. It was great talking to you." Anita had walked three steps to the door when Beth said, "Wait!"

Anita froze peering over her shoulder, eyes round as quarters.

"Didn't you need something when you came in?"

Anita roared with laughter. "I'm sure I came here for something, but got so involved I've forgotten what it was. Oh well, couldn't have been very important."

Beth joined her in laughter. "When you think of it, come on back."

I turned away from the stamp display and hurried after Anita, but got stopped short when the door shut in my face. I made the mistake of glancing at Beth. She stared at me. "May I help you?"

"No. Um. I was checking to see what size mailers you carried. Thanks so much." I grasped the door, pulled it open and scurried out.

Maybe I should take lessons from Anita. Beth probably thought I'd come in to rob the place and lost my nerve.

The motor was running as I jumped into the passenger seat. Anita grinned and backed her mini-van out of the parking space.

I couldn't wait to hear what information she'd obtained. "What did she say? Did she know who owned the box?"

"Yes, and she told me." She beamed. "I asked her about the history of the town. Then I asked if she knew who the first person to rent a box was. She didn't, of course, but she knew the name of the current owner of the first box in the first row—box 101. Aren't we lucky that's the box we needed? I'd have had to ask her to recite all of them. Wonder if she could."

Anita's expression turned stern. "The car is moving, so fasten your seatbelt."

"Okay." I grabbed the belt and locked it in place. Anita liked being in control.

"What's the name?" I tried to lean toward Anita, but found myself secured to the seat.

"Beth remembered because not many of the boxes are rented. Number 101 is Dorene Miller."

"Now we're getting someplace. What's the address?"

"I don't know. Beth didn't have that information. I was trying to figure out how to ask her to look it up when she got into telling me Dorene's life story. I guess she used to be married to Bob Miller, who ran the hardware store before it closed last Spring. Not enough business. Beth said he had no brain for figures and couldn't keep his books straight. They had a messy divorce—not a pretty thing. But now Dorene is dating a nice Italian man from—guess where? Evelynton! She said his name is Mervin or Marvin or Melvin or something. Well, I figured we could find Dorene's address in the phone book. And an Italian man in Evelynton? That shouldn't be too difficult to track down. She was pretty sure his name started with M."

"No need to find a phone book. I'm looking up Doreen's address on my phone."

I dropped the phone in my lap. "Got it."

Chapter Twenty

The town of Harold, Indiana consisted of ten or twelve streets. We drove on most of them searching for the street name and then the house number until we found Dorene Miller's single-story, manufactured home. Anita made a u-turn and parked in front on the street.

Faded red shutters on grimy windows accented the aging white siding. I stepped over a child's well-used blue bicycle on my way to a rickety front porch. The door opened before my fist had hit it the third time.

The woman filling the opening wore baggy jeans and a maroon t-shirt. She stood about my height, but was a few pounds heavier. Her thin brown hair faded to wisps as it reached her shoulders.

"Can I help you?" The monotone voice and unexpressive eyes betrayed the phony smile she wore.

"Hi. I'm Lauren Halloren. I wonder if I can talk to you about hair products." I'd decided last year, after surviving a sticky situation, to be as honest as possible as often as possible.

Dorene squinted at me and answered. "No. I don't want any." Her arm shot out to pull the door shut.

I realized I hadn't explained myself well and stuck out my foot to stop the door. I saw the move on TV. I don't advise it, unless you're wearing reinforced work boots. My sandals didn't offer much protection. "Wait, I'm not selling them. I promise this won't take long."

Dorene glanced down at my foot, and then lifted her gaze to my face. The fake friendly smile had vanished.

I dragged my sore foot back to its place beside the other. "I'm sorry. I didn't mean to be pushy. Just a couple questions. Do you have a post office box?"

My foot throbbed.

"Yes, I have a P.O.Box." She didn't try to hide her impatience. "Whatever you're trying to sell, I don't want any."

"I'm not selling anything. Sorry I haven't been clear." I took a breath and tucked the stricken foot behind the other, taking the weight off it. "Let me explain. A friend of mine purchased some hair color online, and the return address was a post office box I think belongs to you. I just wondered...."

She raised a hand. "Oh, got it."

Her mood changed as if I'd flipped a switch. In an instant she seemed amenable to talking to me and smiled a genuine smile.

"That's my boyfriend. He uses the box for his mother's business. Maybe she sells hair dye, I don't know. He's one of the good guys. Helps his mom whenever he can, so I let him use my box."

I stood on my good foot and leaned against the door frame while Doreen continued. "I can call him if you want to order something. I'm sure he'd love to get more business for her."

That was it. All I needed to know. I was so excited I put my foot down and started to bounce on my toes. Until pain shot up my leg. *Ouch.* "Thank you. I don't think I need anything right now, but maybe later. I just happened to be here in Harold, and thought I'd check it out. I feel it's always good to know who I'm dealing with, don't you agree?" Okay, I'd drifted into storytelling again. I was going to quit that.

"May I ask your boyfriend's name?"

"Mallozi." She giggled. "Don't you try to steal him away."

I laughed and backed away from the porch. "Wouldn't think of it. Thank you for the information."

Sidestepping down the walk, I tripped over the blue bicycle. Then, regaining my footing, I hobbled to the car.

When I'd almost made it, Doreen called out, "Hey, what's your name again? My man will want to know."

I kept my eyes on the car and yanked open the passenger door.

As I climbed in, I ordered, "Hit it, Anita."

She gunned the engine, my door slamming shut as we pulled away from the curb.

"I'm so excited we found the link. Doreen Miller's boyfriend is Mallozi D'agostino. His mother lives across the hall from Louise. Can't believe it was so easy."

Anita took her eyes off the road to look at me. "No kidding? That couldn't be a coincidence. He's absolutely the one who stole from Rarity."

She slowed at a stop sign, then turned onto the highway heading out of Harold. "What an exciting case. I wish you would've let me go up to the door with you. I love this. After we solve this crime and get the publicity, we should form a detective agency. Bet people would flock to us. Wouldn't it be fun?"

"Have you forgotten that last year I almost got shot? I'm glad Doreen didn't see you. She was nice enough and didn't seem dangerous, but we can't be sure. Hope she doesn't remember my name. Pretty sure Doreen's boyfriend is dangerous."

"Lauren, the danger is the fun part. We'll call the agency Danger R Us. Or maybe Danger Girls Detective Agency. Do you think Clair would want to be part of it?"

I slumped into the seat. "No. I don't want to be involved in a detective agency. I'm only doing this because of Rarity."

"Darn." Anita pouted and drove in silence for five minutes while I thought about the case and hoped she would think of other things—like baking pies.

Anita muttered, "Halloren-Corwin Detective Agency. Or if Clair wants in, HCL Agency."

I ignored her until we passed the Evelynton city-limit sign. "Okay, shall I drive straight to the police department?"

"No. I still have to discover how Mallozi gained entrance to The Rare Curl. And I need real evidence of the theft. Maybe some of the stolen goods. Our police force won't listen unless I put it all together for them."

Chapter Twenty-One

I turned off the water and shoved the shower curtain open. My cat sat in the opening, staring up at me. "Move over, Mason. I have things to do."

Instead of making way, he lazily stretched and positioned himself across my path.

"I don't have time for our morning cuddle. I'm meeting Anita and Clair, and I want to stop at the salon first." With my towel wrapped firmly around my chest, I gripped the towel bar and stepped over him. He rolled to his back and pawed my feet as I passed.

"No playing around, I want to have time to talk to Rarity before I meet the girls."

Mason stood and stalked from the room, not to be seen again before I left the house. I think he was mad at me. Or maybe I'd lived alone too long.

~

Rarity sat at the reception desk, pencil in hand, when I poked my head into The Rare Curl. "Good morning, Lauren. How are you this morning? Uh oh. This isn't your day to work is it? My goodness, I'm a day behind. Or am I a day ahead?"

"No, you're not confused. This is my day off. Just stopped in to ask a question."

Rarity sighed and leaned back, sliding the pencil into the mass of red curls above her right ear. "Oh, thank goodness. Hate those senior moments. What do you want to talk about?"

"Just a question. Do we have any customers with the name D'agostino? Maybe Deloris D'agostino?"

"Rings a bell." Rarity scratched her head and repeated the name aloud. Smiling, she said, "Ha. The name rolls off the tongue. Sounds sort of musical, doesn't it. That's probably why I thought it was familiar, but I'm sure we don't have any clients by that name. Why do you ask?"

"No special reason. Deloris is a resident of Beaver Creek, and I wondered if she'd ever had her hair done here. Maybe on my day off. Or what about her son, Mallozi. Does that name ring a bell?"

Rarity shook her head. "No, definitely not. And you know I never forget a customer. That would be like forgetting family."

"I doubt you would forget either of these two. Both have memorable personalities." I swung toward the door. "It isn't important. Just a silly thought."

I glanced over my shoulder as I pushed the door open and stepped through. "On my way to Ava's to meet Clair and Anita. I'll see you tomorrow."

The door had almost closed behind me when Rarity's voice caught my attention. "Lauren. Wait. I remember where I heard that name."

I whirled around and held the door open. Rarity pulled the pencil from her hair and pointed it at me. "That cute young girl who came in asking about becoming a hairdresser. Melody D'agostino. That was her name. It sounds even more melodious than Deloris D'agostino. Sweet girl. Saw our ad in the paper and was curious about the business."

"I remember. We bumped into her the other day on our way out for lunch, didn't we? I bet she's related to the two D'agostinos I know."

"That's the one. She'd never had her hair done here, but I knew the name sounded familiar. Have a nice day and tell Anita the pie she made for the church bake sale was delicious."

It looked as if half of Evelynton had stopped in for coffee at Ava's Java. I waited in line at the counter and scanned the room. Anita and Clair waved from a table near the center of the room.

Accustomed to serving the rush-hour crowd, Ava was adept at passing out the coffee and sweet rolls. Before long, I carried my coffee to join my friends.

I'd just settled into a chair when Anita leaned in, elbows on the table. "I can't wait to hear. Have you discovered the modus operandi?"

Clair gaped at her. "The what?"

"It's detective talk. I asked Lauren if she knew how the thief got in when he stole the stuff from Rarity."

Clair raised her eyes to the ceiling. "So now you're reading crime novels too?"

Anita winked. "Who needs a crime novel? We're having our own adventure."

I caught Clair's eye. "I received a tip the stolen product might be in Harold, Indiana, so Anita and I took a drive there. Got a name and now know who's at the bottom of it. Just didn't know how they got into the salon."

Anita bobbed her head. "Clair, I was about to tell you about our road trip when Lauren came in."

"It all adds up. I know the man from my visits to Beaver Creek. I'm pretty sure the product he sends from that P.O. Box address was stolen from The Rare Curl. I couldn't figure how he got into the salon until a few minutes ago."

Clair laughed. "A guy from the nursing home? He should be easy enough to apprehend. You didn't mention the walker when you told me about seeing the thief during the stakeout."

I leveled my eyes at her until she quit giggling. "He doesn't live there. He's the son of one of the residents."

Forcing the grin from her face, Clair gave me her attention.

"The name I got from the woman in Harold was D'agostino. I just asked Rarity, and she remembered a girl who was in The Rare Curl poking around a few weeks ago. Turns out her name was D'agostino. I think she picked up the extra key at the Rare Curl reception desk."

Clair shook her head. "Did the girl wander around the salon unattended? Why didn't they watch her?"

"She's sweet and very polite. Wouldn't have raised suspicion. In fact, she works here. Have you seen the new girl at the counter some days?"

"You mean the one with the gorgeous thick hair? More than all of us put together? Pretty girl. She's the thief?"

Anita smiled. "Rarity would let anybody wander around the salon if they had a good enough story. Not a suspicious bone in her body."

I took a sip of coffee. "Anita's right. Her name is Melody D'agostino. And she convinced Rarity she wanted to become a hairdresser. But I bet she wasn't so interested in the hair business as she was in Mallozi's business. Rarity said the girl studied the appointment book, so she would have been at the desk. Must have found the key. If Rarity and Stacy were with customers, they wouldn't have watched her."

Anita slapped the table. "That's proof. Let's go get that Mallozi guy. Or maybe we should question the girl first and get her to admit to stealing the key for him."

I leaned my elbow on the table and took a long drink of coffee. "She's young and sweet. Wouldn't want to scare her. I'd agree with confronting Mallozi."

Clair's gaze darted to me, then to Anita, and back to me. "I don't think so, ladies. Go tell the police what you've discovered. Let them handle it. This guy could be trouble. For that matter, so could the girl."

Anita straightened. "The police never listen. At least not to Lauren. We can handle it. You know Lauren has experience."

I cut my eyes to Anita. "Experience? I keep telling you…" I blew out a breath. "Never mind."

I put down my coffee and pushed my hair out of my face with both hands. "Maybe Clair's right. Mallozi as much as warned me off last week when I saw him at the nursing home. At the time I thought he had a personality disorder. You know, wasn't good at relating to people. I think it's more than that."

Anita leaned back and crossed her arms over her chest. "We could do it."

I shook my head. "And remember when I told you that someone chased me through the halls at Beaver Creek? It had to be him."

Clair put a hand on her mouth. "Oh yeah. Sorry I laughed at you. Now that I think about it, sounds like he did it to scare you away from the nursing home."

Anita shifted her gaze from Clair to me, then back again. "I know the three of us could catch him. After all, last year Lauren caught Patsy all by herself."

I clasped my hands to keep from pounding the table. "I did not capture Patsy."

Clair was shaking her head. "Anita, it's time to get the police involved. Lauren had a lucky break when she tackled Patsy."

Did they ever listen to me? "I didn't tackle…. It was Wallace."

Anita's brow furrowed. "You may be right, Clair. Okay, but let's take a day to consider our course of action before we do anything. Maybe we'll come up with a better idea."

Clair slid her chair out. "Well girls, I have to get back to work. Don't do anything without telling me. If you insist on confronting the guy, I'll go with you. And Lauren, dig your gun out of the linen closet. We might need it." She shouldered her bag and made an elegant exit, as only a woman in high heels can.

Anita slid her feet back into her flip-flops. "I'd better get going, too. It's my afternoon at the food pantry. Let's talk tonight."

Chapter Twenty-Two

I paced from the living room to the kitchen. Mason left his food dish and followed me through the dining room. I took it as a willingness to listen to my rant.

"What's my next move? I don't want to go the police. They never believe me. Probably filed our theft report in the "not worth looking at" file. And I definitely don't want to talk to Officer Farlow again."

With a soft meow Mason trotted ahead of me and blocked my path. His golden eyes focused on my face.

I stopped and blew out a breath. "You're right. I should act like a grown-up and report what I know to the authorities. Confronting Mallozi, even with Anita and Clair as backup, would be dangerous. I don't feel right about accusing Melody of stealing the key. I know she probably did. But I'll add that suspicion to the rest and let the authorities deal with it."

Mason lost interest in our conversation when he spotted a fly buzzing by. He took off at a run to apprehend it.

"I give up. I'm going to the police."

~

The office was quiet when I arrived at the Evelynton Police Department. I'd taken time to peek through the door. A few city employees went about their business. No civilians that I could see. I was glad of that, since I didn't know what to expect in response. The department and I had never enjoyed a rapport.

I squared my shoulders and marched in. They would have to listen to me one more time. Maybe they would see the new evidence as an important part of the case. With any luck, Farlow, and his snide remarks, would be out of the office. I could go straight in to see the chief.

I hadn't made it to the counter before I bumped into Officer Farlow. What was that song I'd heard? "If it wasn't for bad luck, I'd have no luck at all."

He let out an overly dramatic sigh. "Ms. Halloren. What do you want?"

I guessed there would be no pleasantries as a warm-up to the conversation. No, nice weather we're having or how's your week?

I plunged in. "I've discovered some information about the theft at The Rare Curl, and I need to report it."

Silly me. I expected him to take me to his desk, maybe pull out his trusty notepad and a pen, but instead I watched him blow out a breath and gaze at a spot above my head. "You discovered information, did you? I don't really have time for your discoveries on the great beauty-shop heist. That hair dye is long gone. It's on some kid's hair and washed down the drain. Mrs. Peabody said so herself. I have better things to do than drag some kid out of class because of a prank."

"It isn't...."

"I've been informed the locks were changed, and there's been no trouble since. Your boss seems happy enough. What's wrong with you?"

I blurted out, "I discovered who stole from Rarity."

"You have conclusive proof?"

I wiped my damp palms on my jeans. "Not absolutely conclusive, but pretty much. It seems obvious to me."

"Ma'am, I don't have time for your daydreams. We have real crime here in Evelynton." Farlow put his hands on his hips and finally looked me in the eye. "If you'll excuse me, I have more important cases to worry about. If you still consider yourself a detective, how about you tell me something new about that dead body you stumbled onto. No, don't tell me. Write it down and put it in the suggestion box."

"I didn't find the body, Clair Lane did. And I don't consider myself a detective. I'd never even think about getting in the middle of that investigation."

Bet I'd be better at it than Farlow.

"I'm glad to hear it, Ms. Halloren. Thought you had your sights set on becoming Evelynton's super hero. Even had yourself a following."

That was uncalled for. "No, I've never considered myself any such thing. But about the salon theft."

Across the room, a phone rang. Farlow looked at it and back at me. "I'm glad you are aware of your tremendous lack of qualification, Ms. Halloren. Let the proper authorities take care of crime in Evelynton."

He poked his finger in my face causing me to take a step back. "I'm telling you. Don't go snooping around where you have no business." The phone continued to ring. Farlow turned on his heel and stalked to his desk.

My mouth fell open as he bellowed from across the room. "If that's all, see yourself out. Goodbye, Ms. Halloren."

He turned his back and snatched the receiver, knocking the cradle off the desk.

I closed my mouth and scanned the room. One police officer smirked as he poured himself a cup of coffee. Irma, the file clerk, kept her attention on the papers she was sorting.

The door was a mere three feet away. *Seemed like a mile.*

Chapter Twenty-Three

I trudged through my front door and slumped onto the sofa. My cat trotted in from the kitchen and stood on his hind legs with front paws on my knee. His luminescent eyes seemed to be filled with sympathy, telling me it would be alright.

I've definitely lived alone too long.

He purred as I stroked his head. "Mason, remind me never to do that again."

I picked up my phone and called Clair to let her know I'd tried to follow her advice and had been laughed out of the building.

Clair listened to my story without interruption and said, "You made the right decision."

I felt vindicated for a moment. Then she continued, "But I can't believe Officer Farlow would be so inconsiderate. You must have caught him on a bad day."

Guess I'd never seen him on a good day. "The man wouldn't listen. He never even gave me the chance to tell him the name of the thief."

"Stay calm, girl. I'm sure he knows best. After all, he is a police officer. And you said the trouble stopped with the change of locks. You're not absolutely positive it was that Mallozi character. Even if it was, when you think about it, he tried to do good. Isn't he sweet for helping his mom? And when he chased you around in the dark, he probably didn't mean to scare you. Some people aren't good at relating to others."

I sucked in a deep breath and exhaled. Couldn't think of anything to say.

"You've done all you could. More than I would have. Aren't you glad it's over? Do something fun today. Something just for you."

I whispered. "It isn't over."

"What was that? Couldn't hear."

"Nothing. It was nothing."

"Anyway, I better get back to work. Talk to you later." A beep sounded, ending the call.

I stomped to the kitchen and nabbed the coffee pot. Cold.

Hrumph.

I put the pot down and stalked to the living room, where I leaned down to pick up my handbag from the floor. Golden eyes gleamed from under the sofa.

"Mason, I'm going to get real evidence. This time the police, especially Officer Farlow, will have to listen."

~

While I steered the Chrysler toward Beaver Creek Rehabilitation Center, I planned my approach. Didn't want to upset Deloris. She was an old lady. At her age, she was probably frailer than she appeared. What would she think when I told her Mallozi was stealing to

138

support her business? Would she have a stroke? A heart attack?

Beaver Creek was quiet when I let myself in. I supposed it was nap time.

I glanced into Louise's room. Empty. Then crossed the hall to Deloris's door.

As usual, she sat in front of the computer.

"Hi, Deloris." No answer. I crept closer and noticed her closed eyelids Quietly, I said, "Deloris?"

An eye popped open and she straightened in her chair. Both eyes open now, she looked at me and smiled.

"Oh, hello, Lauren. I didn't see you there. Been concentrating on this auction."

"Sorry to interrupt you. Louise wasn't in her room, so I thought I'd come over to say hello. How are you?"

"Me? I'm fine. You'll find Louise in Evelyn's Party Room, playing bingo with the other old ladies."

"You didn't want to go? Don't you like bingo?"

"That's for old people with nothing to do. They have plenty of time to waste." She pointed a thumb at her chest. "Me, I have a business to run."

"I can see it takes a lot of your time. It must be fascinating. How are sales?" I stepped closer and strained my eyes to see the computer screen.

Deloris closed her laptop. "My eyes are getting tired from watching the screen. I think I'll let my auctions ride for a while." The big woman heaved herself up from her chair. "Excuse me. I have to go to the powder room."

Deloris lumbered to the bathroom and shut the door.

I stood in silent debate, a tug-of-war between the wise me and the other one—the one that might have worn devil horns. Deloris's computer was so available. She hadn't logged out. Wise me said to back away. The other one, okay, bad me, took over and pushed me closer to the desk. I lifted the screen, and a web page snapped into view.

Couldn't believe my luck. The name of the auction site scrolled across the top of the page. I scanned down until I found Deloris's screen name. A notebook was conveniently located on her desk, so I tore off a page and wrote down the information.

I'd stuffed the page into my pocket when the bathroom door swung open. Deloris stood silhouetted in the bright light of the bathroom. Her short-wide figure, feet apart, one hand on hip, was daunting. She flipped off the bathroom light and came into view. I could see her dark eyes riveted on the laptop, still open.

"What are you doing at my computer? That's my business. It's private. Mallozi warned me to keep it confidential. I don't want anyone stealing my ideas or my customers. He'd be upset with me if he knew you were in here."

"I'm sorry. I wasn't snooping. Sorry if it appeared that way. I was fascinated with how you ran your own business, all from this little room."

The lines deepened and darkened on Deloris's face, and her voice echoed off the walls. "It isn't a little room. This is my home."

I gasped. "Of course. Didn't mean it that way. It isn't little at all, and it's a lovely room, um home. I like it. You have a beautiful view from your window. Much nicer than Louise's"

Deloris glanced out the window, but quickly brought her eyes back to me.

I stammered on. "You know, I only stopped in because Louise wasn't in her room. Thought she might be here with you." I lifted a hand toward the hall. "And, I think she's back. I'll just run over and talk to her. Again, sorry. I couldn't resist taking a peak. That was wrong. But I didn't see anything. Don't even know anything about Internet auctions."

Deloris didn't seem to believe my excuses. She glared as I backed toward the door. I swung around and hurried into the hall.

A gunshot rattled the walls and I dropped to a crouch. Peeking over my shoulder, I realized, it wasn't a gunshot. Deloris had slammed her door.

I glanced up and down the hall to check if there'd been witnesses. There hadn't, so I stood up. Straightening my shirt, I sauntered toward the exit in an attempt at a dignified exit.

Out on the sidewalk, I wanted to slap myself on the head. After Deloris's outburst, I'd forgotten the reason for the visit. Someone needed to tell Deloris of Mallozi's illegal scheme. The poor woman would be crushed, but a broken heart would be better than landing in jail.

I glanced back at the nursing home. Couldn't go back in there. Best to go home and check out the meager information I'd found. Then with more evidence, I'd ask Rarity to go with me. She was an expert at talking to people, especially women like Deloris.

~

Back at the house, I looked up the Internet site and found Deloris's auctions. There were dozens in progress, with timers ticking away on each one. Almost every sale featured hair color. None of the auctions listed the brand-name but I could see it on the bottles pictured. I printed screen shots of most of her items and called Rarity.

"I'm on my way over to show you something. I know where your hair color has gone. And it wasn't teenagers."

"You're still investigating, Lauren? I'd almost forgotten about it. If you think it's important, I'll look at what you have."

It took fifteen minutes to get to Rarity's house, and ten minutes later she agreed with me.

Rarity picked up her purse. "Poor Mrs. D'agostino. It will be heartbreaking for her to learn about her son's poor judgment. But it would be much worse if he gets her into trouble with the law. There's no time to waste. Who knows what else he might be doing? And involving his elderly mother."

With relief, I opened the door for her. "I'll drive. You can plan how you'll break the news."

"Me?" Rarity stared at me for a moment. "I guess you're right. I should be the one to tell her. But let's take my VW. It was nice of your aunt to leave you the Chrysler, but I worry how long it will continue to run. Let's not put any more miles on it than necessary."

I'd grown accustomed to the old station wagon. A luxury car in its day, the thirty-six-year-old vehicle now drove like a tank and took all my strength to maneuver it.

"Thank you. I'd love to ride in your bug."

Chapter Twenty-Four

I punched in the code to open the door at Beaver Creek and led the way in. The usual cluster of residents, up from their naps, held onto walkers and sat in wheelchairs inside.

Employing my usual method of entering, I smiled, but scooted through quickly. Having escaped to the other side of the mob, I noticed Rarity in the center, being treated like a celebrity. She greeted each senior, while I leaned against the wall and waited.

The first in line was a little man with about four hairs combed across his shiny head. "Hello, John. Haven't seen you for a while. How have you been? How's your son? And your grandkids?"

She moved to another man and took his hand. "Hello. I'm Rarity. Did you say your name was Arthur? How's it going?"

I had no idea what Arthur said, but Rarity listened to every indecipherable word. It took a full three minutes.

Still holding his hand, she said, "I'm sorry to hear that, Arthur. But I'm so glad your back is better. I'm sure the doctors will do a fine job in fixing your hip."

That seemed to be the end of it until a tiny-fuzzy-haired woman scooted forward to claim Rarity's attention. She absorbed each faint whisper with grave attention.

"It's so nice to meet you, Gladys. Sometimes it's good to have a roommate. Don't take it as a bad thing. I think you'll find it's nice to have someone around to share the little things with."

Rarity raised her head and saw me waiting patiently. At least, I hoped I appeared patient.

She spoke to the group. "I have to go. You probably know my friend, Lauren. We are on an important mission today. So nice to meet all of you." She smiled, squeezed hands, and even blew kisses as she extricated herself from her clutch of admirers.

We walked into the lobby. "Sorry to keep you waiting, Lauren."

"Not a problem. But could you understand what that little man and the last lady were saying?"

"No, hardly any of it, but they needed to talk. My agenda would never be more important than listening. Now, where's Deloris's room?"

"Down this hall. I hope she's in her room. If not, we'll have to go looking."

We found Deloris D'agostino stretched out in her recliner, slippered feet propped up.

I tapped on the open door. "Hi, Deloris. May we come in? I want to apologize again for the misunderstanding the other day. I wouldn't snoop and I would never want to make Mallozi angry."

"It's okay, as long as he doesn't find out. I probably overreacted. Mallozi said I do that."

"This is my friend and boss, Rarity Peabody."

Before I finished my introduction, Rarity was holding Deloris's hand. The two behaved like old friends. Should've known Rarity would take control of the situation. "I love the comforter on your bed. Such vivid colors. Red is my favorite. And that geometric design is so interesting."

Deloris's eyes sparkled and her cheeks grew rosy. "I'm glad you like it. My family wanted to get me something in pink, but I told them I wasn't going to be like all the old people. I want everything cheerful."

"I know exactly what you mean. Sometimes the kids want you to fit into their perception of a given age. So glad you're intent on living an interesting life."

Deloris absorbed the praise with the first heart-felt smile I'd seen on her.

Then Rarity employed a segue so smooth I wanted to write it down for future reference.

"And Lauren tells me you're running your own business. That's wonderful. Adjusting to your surroundings and making the best of it. You are an inspiration."

While Deloris was basking in the shower of praise, Rarity got down to business. "That's why I wanted to talk to you. There's something I'm sure you aren't aware of. I needed to tell you, one mother to another."

Deloris tipped her head and leaned closer to Rarity. "What is it?"

"I think your son, in his very admirable desire to help you, is making a mistake in obtaining the items you sell."

Deloris leaned back and gripped the arms of her chair. "I don't understand. What do you mean by a mistake?"

"Well dear, I'm afraid he has obtained your products by illegal means, probably by mistake, through no fault of his own. It turns out that the hair color you sell in your auctions isn't supposed to be sold to the public. The supply house I use tells me there's no way a reputable dealer would supply the product to anyone but a licensed salon, and never for Internet auction. In fact, items just like the ones you're selling were stolen from my salon."

A deeper flush of color began to cover Deloris's cheeks, and Rarity hastened to reassure her. "Oh, I didn't mean Mallozi stole them. Whoever sold them to him probably did. Don't worry, Deloris. I know you had no idea, and I'm sure your son didn't know what he was doing. It's all a little accident that is easily fixed. He'll just have to find something else for you to sell. You are such a good businesswoman, I know it will be easy for you to adjust."

Deloris sat straight up in her chair, her breathing verging on labored. Her eyes scanned the room from one side to the other. "I can't believe it. I had no idea. He'd never do anything illegal. Someone's taking advantage of my Mallozi."

With a hand on Deloris's shoulder, Rarity nodded. "I'm sure that's it. But don't worry. I wanted you to know so you wouldn't get into trouble."

Rarity gazed at Deloris. "I've upset you. And I'm sorry. Take slow, deep breaths."

Even Rarity's soothing tone of voice failed to calm the big woman. Deloris's jaw set with clenched teeth. Her breathing accelerated. "You better go. Go!"

Rarity stood and backed out of the room. "I assure

you it's going to be alright. If you would have a word with your son, I'm sure everything will be fine. Just a simple mistake."

Deloris raised a stout arm and pointed to the door. "Out!"

Rarity's eyes were big and round when they met mine. We spun around to escape through the door.

While we scurried down the hall, Rarity whispered. "Poor Deloris seemed to take the news hard. The sweet thing was so upset. She's worried about her boy. Do you think she'll be alright?"

I thought she might explode. "I'll ask a nurse to look in on her to make sure she calms down."

Helen was sitting at her desk so we stopped to explain the situation. Well, not the whole situation. I shortened it to "Deloris seemed agitated. You might want to check on her."

Chapter Twenty-Five

Y uk." I'd rolled over into a face-full of cat fur. "Mason, get off my pillow." I spit out cat hair as I answered the ringing telephone.

"Morning."

"Sorry to call so early, Lauren. It's Rarity. I just got off the phone with Mrs. D'agostino."

"Deloris? I didn't think she'd ever speak to us again."

"The poor thing was in tears, thinking Mallozi would get into trouble. She said she didn't sleep all night for the worry."

I shook my head to clear the hairball "I don't understand why she called you. How'd she even get your number?"

"Don't know. She probably asked someone at Beaver Creek. But she spoke to Mallozi and they figured out how the mix-up happened. It turns out we have it wrong. The hair color on her site was off-brand and came from a swap meet or rummage sale Mallozi found in Indianapolis. He knew she'd love to sell it so he picked up a whole crate."

"But remember we saw the products in the pictures. They were professional products. Just like yours."

"Oh, Deloris explained that too. Mallozi couldn't take clear photographs of the actual items he brought, so he gathered pictures from the Internet. You know, being the sweet boy he is, he put in the extra effort. Deloris promised to have him change all the photos to those of the actual bottles."

I pushed Mason off the bed and slid my feet into sandals. "Sounds sort of convenient to me. But you believe their story?"

"I do. Let's let the whole thing drop. You saw how upset the poor woman was when we left. I was afraid she'd had a heart attack."

"Okay. Whatever you say."

I was not convinced, but Rarity had already jumped to another subject. "I'm calling a window washer today. I think our front display needs to be updated for the late summer season, don't you?"

"Mmm. Sure."

"And I'm interviewing a hairdresser, too. On the phone, she sounded like she'd fit right in."

My brain was ticking away, even without coffee.

"You know, Rarity, it could easily be proved."

"What could be proved?"

"About the hair color. If Deloris would supply names of her customers. We could contact a few of them and ask to see the bottles."

"Lauren Grace. We must show mercy to this poor woman. I know you mean well, but let's not bother her again. I refuse to distress Deloris any more. Promise me you'll forget all about it. I know you just want to help me, but you're mistaken about this."

"Okay. I promise I won't question Deloris."

"Wonderful. I knew you'd understand. Well I must get on with my day. You have a pleasant morning."

I hung up.

Mallozi was lying. He was a crook, and he'd deceived his mother. Why didn't Rarity see it? It would be better for Deloris to remedy the situation quickly and get it over with. What might Mallozi do next? What if he stole from someone not as nice as Rarity? Deloris would wind up in jail along with her son. Now that would distress the woman.

I stomped to the kitchen, pulled out a can of coffee and began measuring the grounds into the pot.

Mallozi might fool his mother, but he didn't fool me. I couldn't believe Rarity fell for his story.

How many scoops of coffee had I added to the pot? I threw in another, to be safe.

While the coffee brewed, I leaned on the counter. "There must be a way to contact Deloris's customers. Where do I find her records? I don't remember a file cabinet in her room. What do you think, Mason?"

Where was the cat?

Talking to myself again.

I took my coffee to the living room, but did an about-face when I passed the computer. Mason lay curled up on the keyboard.

"Mason, the computer is not a bed. Off you go." I gave him a nudge with two fingers.

After a complaining meow, he stepped from the keyboard to an open spot on the desk.

"Yuk." Black and white hairs were strewn through the keys. They filled the air when I blew on them.

That's when I noticed the screen. An assortment of Internet sites had been opened. "Mason, what did you do?"

I began clicking the little X on each web page. A social network site—closed. A news site—closed. My email account—closed. An auction site.

"Mason, w at a dunce I've been. Deloris's customer records would be kept on the site, not on paper. All I have to do is discover how to get into her account. How do I find her account log-in information?"

The cat leapt from the desk and left the room, tail held high.

"Some friend you are."

I stared at the monitor. What would an old lady use as a password? If she was anything like me, she would have written it down somewhere. I'm young—comparatively—and all my passwords are written on a pad of paper I keep hidden away. The point being that even though we have been warned not to write down passwords, we do.

Or she might have the computer remember her password for the site. That would be much easier for an old lady to handle. All I had to do was get to her computer. If she was out of her room and the door wasn't locked, no problem.

Chapter Twenty-Six

The corridors were empty. I'd made a point of walking into Beaver Creek at lunch time in hopes Deloris had chosen that day to eat her meal in the dining room. If she had, I'd have an hour. Easy to get in and get out without being seen.

I'd also counted on her still being logged in to her computer. It occurred to me that I depended on a lot of sheer luck to make this work.

First, I took a leisurely stroll past the dining room and peeked in. Deloris sat a table on the far side of room with a full plate. I congratulated myself on my first bit of luck.

I hurried back past the door and trotted to her room. The door wasn't locked. Second bit of luck.

The computer was open.

"Yes!" I was doing well in the luck department.

If she was still logged in to the auction site, I'd do a happy dance.

It took me a few minutes to find the website. Her information automatically filled the blanks. I clicked the log-in button and I was in. I almost shrieked,

"Hooray." But I clasped my hand over my mouth and settled into the desk chair.

Opening tabs and clicking buttons, I navigated the site and found her buyer files. I'd reached for her notepad when I heard voices in the hall. The voices weren't soft and pleasant. They were the voices of a mother and son in heated conversation.

"Mallozi, I don't know why you had to come right at lunch time. We had chicken pot pie. I wasn't finished."

"Ma, you had plenty to eat. We needed to talk and I don't have much time. Have to get back to work."

I sprang up from the computer and hurried to the door. Too late to slip out unseen. Deloris and Mallozi had turned the corner and would reach the room within seconds.

Now what did I get myself into? I looked toward the bed, picturing the dust bunnies that would probably be under it.

The bathroom was the only other place large enough for me to hide. I ran in and pulled the door closed.

After realizing there was only one way out of my hiding place, I knew I hadn't made the best decision. How long could I stay there? I prayed they would finish their argument and Deloris would go back to her chicken pot pie.

Mallozi's bellowing was loud enough to vibrate the door. "I told you. You weren't supposed to sell to anyone in this county. You had plenty customers in other states, even other countries. You only had to follow a couple simple rules. Don't sell close, and keep your mouth shut about it."

Deloris replied and I knew where Mallozi got his temper. "Don't yell at me, I'm your mother. Besides, I followed your stupid rules, and you know it. You sent all of my deliveries. Didn't you look at the addresses? I didn't give anyone in Evelynton any product. Even though I could have made a lot of money right here at Beaver Creek. All these old, gray-haired people. Could've have been set for life. But you wanted privacy."

"Then you must have told someone. How did they know? You should've listened to me, Ma. All you had to do was keep your lips sealed."

"Don't you accuse me. I brought you into this world." Ah, the mom card.

Their argument was entertaining, if I overlooked my own predicament. But the row sounded like it could last for a while, so I closed the lid on the bathroom toilet and sat down.

Mallozi's frustration seemed to be growing. "No disrespect, Ma, but you messed up somehow. I kept everything straight on my side. I even taught Melody exactly what to say.

"Ha. Told you she was too young. Maybe she told."

"No, Ma. She didn't know what was going on, so I know it wasn't her. She didn't have anything to tell. Think about it. Who'd you tell?"

"I did everything right. The mistake was on your end."

Heavy footsteps approached my hiding place. My heart pounded, and I stared at the door and held my breath, waiting for it to open. The sound of the steps receded, and I sucked in oxygen.

The argument seemed to be wearing on Mallozi. His voice lowered. "I've done everything for you, even took care of Camden."

"Camden? Oh, that nice friend of yours. I liked him. Where's he been? He used to come see me once in a while."

"Don't kid me, Ma. You know where he's been."

Deloris's voice took on an almost girlish quality. "I don't know what you mean. I miss him, but I suppose he's been too busy to visit an old lady."

"What are you talking about? Some of the loonies in this place have lost their memory, but yours is as sharp as it ever was."

Deloris's voice exuded exaggerated sweetness, even through the bathroom door. "Oh, I remember. He died, didn't he? Poor boy. That's what you meant when you said you took care of him."

Deloris's tone changed. No more girlish voice. "Ha. As soon as I read it in the newspaper, I knew what you'd done. How could you leave him just lying there in the woods? Why didn't you bury him?"

"I don't like to dig, Ma. You know that. My bad back."

"Yeah, you were never built for physical labor. But I thought you were smarter. Left him in the open. You had to know they'd find him. And now it's only a matter of time until they link Camden to you. You two worked for the same company."

It sounded as if Mallozi's fist hit the wall, or maybe it was his head. Either way, he was becoming frustrated with his mother. "I didn't leave him out in the open. Pulled him all the way into the woods. It wasn't easy. I thought out there in the briers, he'd be buried in

155

sticks and leaves by winter. How did I know those women would stumble on his body before all the leaves came down? What were they doing, snooping around out there? I hate snoops."

Snoops? I'm not a snoop. I'm curious.

All I heard for the next few minutes was the sound of footsteps pacing in the next room. Then there was a loud squeak I attributed to Deloris sitting in the recliner.

Deloris's voice turned soft. Was the argument almost over? "You know I love my business. Now that that newspaper woman is on to you, I'll lose my source of income."

I wanted to storm out of the bathroom to tell her I'm not a newspaper woman.

"Ma, you won't lose your business. I'll fix it."

I sucked in a breath. *Fix it?* Like he fixed Camden?

The room was quiet once more. I got up and pressed my ear against the door, straining to hear past my own breathing.

Then there was sound, but not what I wanted to hear. A squeak from the recliner, and the sound of shuffling feet. I knew Deloris approached the door on which my ear was pressed.

Uh-oh. Now what?

Wildly searching for another place to hide, my eyes stopped at the only sanctuary. I climbed into the bathtub and slipped behind the shower curtain. My knees shook so badly I thought I'd collapse. Fortunately, there was a shower chair sitting in the tub, so I took a seat and waited.

The bathroom door creaked as it opened.

I closed my eyes and prayed to be invisible.

Deloris's voice bounced off the ceramic walls.

"Mallozi!"

It was both deafening and disheartening.

The next sound was worse. Heavy footsteps brought Mallozi into the room.

The shower curtain flung back, revealing my sanctuary. I peered out like a frightened deer.

Mallozi loomed over me. "It's you. What're you doing in here?"

It's difficult to appear innocent while sitting on a shower chair in a bathtub belonging to someone else. "Um. This is embarrassing, but I had to go to the bathroom and ran in here. It was the closest because Louise was using hers. Then I heard you come in. And you were having a serious conversation, so I didn't want to interrupt so I sat down here to wait."

"Ma, she heard everything we said."

Deloris squeezed in beside Mallozi at the open shower curtain. The two of them took up most of the space, and nearly all of the oxygen in the bathroom.

Trapped in the bathtub. No place to run. I'd have to talk my way out.

I shook my head. "Oh no. I didn't mean I listened to you. You were having a serious conversation so I made a point of not listening. " I looked from one to the other. Were they buying it?

Deloris pointed a finger at me. "That isn't true. You're a newspaper reporter, and you were snooping."

"I'm not a reporter, I'm..."

Mallozi interrupted me. "The walls in this place are paper-thin. You heard every word. I hate snoops." He swiveled his head to his mother, who was glaring down at the snoop sitting on her shower chair. "Ma. Now we've got trouble."

The air thinned so much I felt dizzy.

To my great relief, Mallozi backed up and pulled Deloris from the bathroom. "Turn on the TV and turn up the volume. Then check the hallway to see if anyone's around."

I'd clambered out of the tub and made it as far as the door when Mallozi blocked my exit. I attempted to raise my voice above the blaring television. "No, really. I only heard a word here and there. Don't know what you were talking about. I felt terrible being there. So embarrassing."

Maybe I could change the mood by appearing casual. I crossed my arms and leaned on the door frame.

Mallozi and Deloris stood between me and freedom, and they didn't buy my innocent routine.

Deloris wrung her hands and whined. "This is terrible. My business."

"She's the only one who knows. You can keep your business if she goes away."

I shouted. "Goes away? That's what I'm doing right now. I'll be going. I really have to find Louise."

Would anyone hear me above the television noise?

Mallozi leaned forward and stared at me with his beady eyes. He took a step closer. From his posture, I might be in for a head-butt.

I prayed for intervention—any kind of intervention. Right away would be good.

There came a loud rapping at the door, causing all three of us to jump. Hallelujah, someone very large— maybe a security guy.

Mallozi looked at his mother and then at the door. He grabbed the knob and inched it open only far enough for him to see out. I crept forward and squinted through the crack to see a tiny, white-haired lady in a pink dress. Louise had come to the rescue. My spirits crashed. I'd have to practice being more specific in prayer.

I was wrong. The little old lady leaned into the door, and shoved with all the might her four-foot-tall, ninety-pound body could muster. Caught by surprise and thrown off balance, Mallozi stumbled backwards. The door flung all the way open, sending him to the floor.

Louise brightened. "Oh, there you are, Lauren. I've been looking for you. Why don't you come down to the dining room with me? I'd love the company."

Mallozi rolled around on the floor, attempting to get to his feet. He stammered something about me staying, but I'd leaped over him, and was at the door.

I looped my arm around Louise, lifting the tiny woman off the floor. We crossed the corridor where I deposited her in her room. "Lock the door and don't open it!"

After I'd pulled her door shut, I took off at a run.

At the reception area, I searched for a nurse or an aide. None in sight. A few elderly residents sat in the hallway. Not wanting to upset them, I pulled up and quick-walked to the front door. As soon as I pushed through the exit, I launched into a full run. There seemed to be no one around to help. I ran down the sidewalk and turned the corner at the end of the building. There, I slammed into an immovable object, knocking the air from my lungs. I tipped up my chin and looked up into dark, smoldering eyes that held a tinge of surprise. Jack.

My plea was weak. "Help."

Within a few seconds, Mallozi barreled around the corner after me, only to become acquainted with the afore-mentioned immovable object. Jack raised his right arm and grabbed the shorter man by his shirt collar.

Mallozi struggled, but Jack easily detained him. I relaxed and leaned against Jack.

His voice, stern but calm, would have frightened the worst of criminals into submission. "Why are you chasing Ms. Halloren?"

While he tried in vain to release Jack's fingers from his shirt, Mallozi sputtered. "Hey, that woman broke into my mom's room, and was rummaging through her things."

Jack looked at me.

I shook my head.

"What's going on, Lauren?"

"He's the killer. The body Clair and I found in the woods. Mallozi killed him. I heard him admit it to his mother. Um, I was in Deloris's room searching for clues to the thefts at The Rare Curl. You see, Mallozi stole the merchandise and gave it to Deloris to sell in online auctions. Anyway, they surprised me while I was searching, so I hid in the bathroom. While I was in there, I heard him admit the murder."

Mallozi reached out to grab me, but his hand fell short. I shifted closer to Jack's other side, under the protection of his left arm.

"Tell the police to check on a man named Camden, who worked with Mallozi. They'll find out, he's missing and they have his body in the morgue. It was him we found on the trail."

Jack blinked. "Go on."

"I bet Camden and Mallozi committed the thefts at The Rare Curl and gave the stuff to Deloris. Then Mallozi killed Camden."

"Who's Deloris?" Jack tipped his head to the side to look me in the eyes.

"Deloris is Mallozi's mother. She lives in Beaver Creek."

Mallozi wiggled, trying to get out of Jack's grip. He sputtered, "That crazy woman's lying. She's made up some absurd story. I should call the police."

With Mallozi still dangling from his fist, Jack sighed. "Good idea. Why don't we all take a trip down to the station and let them sort it out."

Mallozi stopped thrashing. "I may have over-reacted. No reason for you to be involved. I'll let it go this time. Don't want to upset my Ma."

Jack turned his head to look into Mallozi's eyes. "You'll let it go? I caught you chasing my girl. I won't let that go."

My girl?

I gazed up at Jack, aware I might have had a silly smile on my face.

"Lauren, is that your wagon over there? You drive. I'll sit in the back with our friend here."

"Um. Okay." Reluctantly stepping out of the warm spot next to Jack, I pulled my keys from my pocket and crossed the walk to my car. After I'd climbed in and prepared to start the engine, I noticed Jack and Malozi waiting outside the back door. Jack pointed to the door handle.

"Oops." I stretched over the seat back to pull up the lock. "Sorry. Really need get a car with automatic locks."

I drove to the police department trying to keep my eyes on the road. The temptation to stare at Jack through the rear-view mirror was almost too much to resist.

We marched up the steps. Police officers turned to stare as we entered.

Jack placed his hand on my back and leaned close. "Stay here. I'll be right back." He walked into the chief's office, dragging Mallozi along with him. After a few minutes the chief stepped out.

"Officer Farlow, put Mr. D'agostino in a cell, and then take Ms. Halloren's statement."

I beamed, straightened my shoulders and walked to Farlow's desk, expecting Jack to follow me. When I sensed he wasn't behind me, I whipped my head around toward the door. My rescuer stood with his hand on the handle.

"Jack?"

"All taken care of. I'll see you later." And he stepped out.

"What do you mean, 'all taken care of'? Where are you going?" Jack didn't hear me. He'd closed the door and was gone.

Even though Officer Farlow was surprisingly polite as I gave him my statement, I couldn't wait to get out of there. Thirty minutes later I climbed into the Chrysler and guided it into traffic toward home.

The events of the day scrolled through my mind.

Crap.

I slammed on the brakes and cranked the steering wheel, making a three-point turn in an intersection. Ignoring the shaking fists of the two drivers who had been behind me, I drove back the way I'd come.

As soon as I'd parked at Beaver Creek, I rushed to Louise's room and tapped on the door. Not sure she heard it for the racket from inside, I raised my voice. "Louise, it's me."

The lock released, and the door opened a crack. Pale blue eyes peeked out, and then the door opened all the way. Louise stood in the doorway holding her reading lamp, cord dangling. "Hello Lauren. I'm relieved to see you unharmed."

"Almost forgot you, Louise. Things happened so fast, I didn't have time to come back and let you know we were taking Mallozi to jail."

"Oh, no problem, dear. I prayed for your safety. And it was time for my program, so I figured I'd watch it while I waited." She indicated a game show blaring away on her television.

"What's with the lamp?"

"It's my weapon. Couldn't think of anything else that might work. Guess I can put it back beside my bed."

"I'll do it."

Ten minutes later, as I turned to leave, a police officer stood at Deloris's door.

Her voice had turned girlish again. "Officer, I can't believe my boy did it. I guess Mallozi got in with the wrong crowd. You know the younger generation. I'm just an old lady. Only have this little room."

I walked quietly down the hall and left the building.

Chapter Twenty-Seven

I'd been up a whole five minutes and stood at the kitchen counter staring at the coffee pot, counting on will power to make the coffee brew faster. The ringing telephone made me jump. When my heart slowed, I lifted the handset.

"Lauren!" I held the phone away from my ear.

"Good morning, Clair. You don't have to talk so loud. I can hear you."

"Oops. Sorry. I just heard the exciting news and had to talk to you."

"I don't know if I'm ready for such excitement. What news did you hear?"

"What else? That you are a hero again. Just called to congratulate you. Irma, my contact at the police station, phoned to fill me in. Can't believe you did it again."

I shielded my eyes from the sunlight streaming in the kitchen window. "What did I do again?"

"Don't be coy. You know you caught the thief-slash-murderer and helped identify the body we found. It was your info that led the police to Mallozi

D'agostino's workplace, The Warehouse Buyers Club. Irma said you provided the first name, Camden, and they discovered Camden Green hadn't shown up for work in a while. He and D'agostino were buddies. The police think they'll have a positive ID within a week."

I tried to stifle a yawn, hoping Clair wouldn't notice.

"You're amazing. So brave."

I poured a cup of coffee and sat at the table. I wasn't ready for such enthusiasm so early in the morning.

"I'm not brave, and I didn't catch anyone. What I did was nearly get myself killed."

"Oh, I almost forgot. Not only did you solve the small-time theft at The Rare Curl, but uncovered major theft from the warehouse."

"What major theft? I don't know anything about any major theft."

"Whether you knew about it or not, you got the credit. It seems that after the police called the warehouse, the manager checked the inventory. They're missing a lot of appliances and cash from the safe. The police don't know how D'agostino and Green unloaded the merchandise yet. Probably shipped them out of state. It was all because you insisted on investigating Rarity's missing hair color. Girl, you should change careers. You're a born detective."

"No, that is not the career for me. In fact, I needed to be rescued. If Ja…"

Clair wasn't listening. "D'agostino admitted to the thefts, but denied killing Green. Probably thought he'd confess to the lesser crime and beat the murder charge. But Chief Stoddard's determined to prove him guilty on both counts. He thinks Green may have wanted a bigger cut, or maybe even threatened to turn D'agostino in."

I let Clair talk so I could drink coffee.

"Imagine, Mallozi involved his own mother in the crime. That's despicable. The poor woman's life was turned upside down. Her son in jail, and her little business ruined. I want to do something nice for her."

"That's kind of you, but be careful. She's very protective of Mallozi. When Rarity and I went to see her, thinking we were being helpful, she ordered us out of the room. Didn't want to hear he might be involved in anything illegal. We thought she'd have a stroke."

"When you think about it, that was sweet. She wanted to protect her little boy, even though he's a grown man. She doesn't know who I am, but I'll send her flowers. Let her know that people of Evelynton care."

I swallowed the last drops in my coffee mug and got up to refill it. "You're right, Deloris deserves compassion. Anyone her age should be able to live peacefully, not have to deal with a law-breaking son. I'll check in on her when I visit Louise. Maybe she'd like company."

"Great. You'll have lots of time now that you've finished the investigation."

"I wouldn't call it lots of time. I'll be catching up on magazine articles to support myself."

"Speaking of supporting oneself, I'm off to show a house. Talk to you later, girl. And again, congratulations, my hero."

I clicked off the phone. Enough of the "my hero" stuff. No, I definitely wasn't cut out to be a detective.

When I'd first returned to Evelynton, I remember

thinking how bored I would be living here. Now I was thankful my hometown would soon return to the quiet little burg it used to be.

Chapter Twenty-Eight

Sunshine and bird songs interrupted my writing. Couldn't concentrate. It was the kind of day that begged for a lazy drive in the country. One of the things I'd learned to appreciate in small-town living was the ability to get out of town without fighting traffic. I yearned to drive through the country fields with no distractions.

I guess I should have chosen another route out of town. I made the mistake of driving past the police station. A woman climbed the handicap ram on her mobility scooter. A woman with black hair and white roots, whose width was the same as her height. Clair's word rang through my mind. Deloris must be devastated. She'd lost the business she was so proud of and was about to lose her son to prison.

I parked the Chrysler on the street and waited for her to finish with her visit to Mallozi. When the scooter appeared in the doorway, I jumped out of the Chrysler and trotted over.

"Deloris, I'm glad I happened to see you. Wanted to tell you how sorry I was about Mallozi. It must have been very hard for you to see your son in jail. I hope you understand, someone had to stop him. His crime might have spilled over onto you. I didn't want you to end up in jail as well."

Deloris raised her head to look at me. Her eyes grew wide and her nostrils flared. My first thought was retreat, and fast. But her anger faded. "Couldn't believe my boy would do anything against the law, but the police chief said they had proof. It's good Mallozi was caught. Now he will get help. I don't blame you. It was his own doing. When he gets out of jail, he'll get on with his life. He can still have a good life."

"I'm glad you understand." Maybe she didn't really understand. If they proved he was a killer, like I thought they would, he'd be in jail for a long time. Getting on with his life would mean getting used to prison.

I thought of Clair's determination to do something for Deloris. "If there is anything I can do for you, just ask. I'd be happy to help."

Deloris guided her scooter down the sidewalk and shouted, "Walk with me back to Beaver Creek. It's a long way and I don't want to be alone."

"Oh sure, I'd love to, but why don't I call Beaver Creek and ask them to send a van to pick you and your scooter up?"

"No, I don't want to bother them. Besides, they don't need to know my business."

I glanced back at my station wagon. "Sure. I'll walk with you."

"Good. Come on." Deloris began to motor down the street.

"It's a nice day for a walk. Not too hot." I waited

for Deloris to respond. When she didn't I tried again. "It's so nice you have your scooter, so you can enjoy the outdoors."

I guess she wasn't interested in small talk. Maybe she didn't hear me, since the distance between us was increasing.

I had to step up the pace to keep up with her. By the end of the next block, she had the pedal flush with the metal, and I struggled to keep up. "Wow. Didn't know motorized chairs had so much power." I fell behind again and jogged to catch her.

Clair would have been proud of me. I alternated the power walk and jog, to stay with Deloris until we arrived at Beaver Creek.

Leaning on the railing to catch my breath, I strained to get the words out. "Here we are. I'm glad I could accompany you on your ride home. And so thankful you don't blame me for Mallozi's arrest. I'll be going back now."

I punched the button that opened the door for Deloris. She stopped at the entrance. "Don't go yet. Come in and talk to me. We never got to know each other well, and I'm going to need friends now that I don't have my son to visit me."

"Of course. It would be great getting to know you."

I wiped sweat from my forehead. "I could use the rest before I walk back to my car, anyway."

Deloris drove her scooter to the foot of her bed and plugged the cord into the outlet.

I fell into a chair, wondering if I should prepare the woman for her son going to prison for murder. Would it be better to know beforehand or to be caught off guard? I would want to be prepared.

I plunged in, hoping that stating the truth quickly would be less painful. "Deloris, I have something to say, and I say it only to save you a shock later on. Do you understand they suspect Mallozi of killing Camden Green? I'm afraid they will charge him with murder. If they find him guilty, he may be in jail for the rest of his life."

Deloris glared at me and shook her head. "I don't want to talk about it." She swung her feet to the floor, lumbered off the scooter, and shuffled toward her dresser.

I'd upset her, but at least she wouldn't be blindsided.

"Do you have any other family in town? I could call them for you."

"My brother and his kids, but we don't talk."

This touched my heart. The poor woman was estranged from her family, and now her son was in jail. She had no one.

"I remember. I met Melody D'agostino. Is she related?"

"Yeah, one of my brother's grandkids. Mallozi knows her. I don't know any of them."

"Would you like me to call them? I bet they'd want to know and would come to be with you."

Deloris had reached the dresser. She propped both hands on it for support. She shifted her head toward at me, and snapped. "I bet they'd like to know. Nosy people. But they don't need to know my business."

"Sorry, I didn't realize. So, I won't contact them. But you have friends here at Beaver Creek. Louise enjoys talking to you."

"Yeah, I guess so."

The conversation did little to elevate her mood. I sat in silence and let my mind wander. Not a good thing because that lets my curiosity come out. I'd been warned that someday it would get me into trouble.

"Deloris, why do you think Mallozi would have killed Camden Green? I mean, if he did kill him. Do you think it had anything to do with your business?"

Deloris pulled open a drawer and twisted toward me. She held a very large Glock. "I told you I don't want to talk about it."

My voice caught in my throat and I squeaked. "Oh my. That's the biggest pistol I've ever seen. Careful. Don't aim it at me."

She stared at me with the weapon aimed directly at my chest. If I'd wanted to help the woman feel better, it appeared I'd succeeded. She looked calmer than I'd ever seen her, even weating a slight smile.

I struggled to find the words to keep her in conversation. "That gun is huge. Isn't it heavy?"

"I'm a big woman. I use big tools."

"I don't understand. Why are you pointing that at me?"

Deloris breathed out a sigh. "I told you I didn't want to talk about the products I sold. Just like I told Camden to shut up about my business. Now I'm telling you."

"Wait. I don't know what you mean, but I promise I'll shut up. I don't need to know. My stupid curiosity always gets the best of me."

The woman made no sign of hearing me. "Camden was easy. He took a walk with me. Followed just like a puppy. Right into the alley behind the drugstore. He sure was surprised when I pulled out my Glock. This is going to be a bit trickier."

She waved the gun around a little bit as she spoke. I flinched, wondering when it would go off.

"That wimp said he was afraid the warehouse was suspicious of him and Mallozi. He didn't want to get caught, so we had to stop, or he would turn in my boy."

The old woman continued to wave the barrel of the gun. "Deloris, I wish you wouldn't talk with your hands. It's sort of dangerous.

She paid no attention. "I knew where the goods came from. Did you think I was a dummy? You all misjudge older people. Camden thought I was a pushover. He wanted out. Threatened to tell the police if we went on with it. I told him I wouldn't close my business. In fact I'd increase it. I'd have Mallozi share some of the big stuff from the warehouse."

"You're a good businesswoman."

Deloris made a face. "Such a baby. Camden freaked out and said he was pulling the plug on the whole caper. He said he cared about me so was telling me first. Didn't want me to get into trouble. He thought I'd appreciate the kindness."

She shook the gun at me. "Just like you."

I scanned the room for a place to hide. Would the recliner stop a bullet? Probably not. Deloris had a really big gun.

"Camden would have spoiled everything. So I led him to the alley, pulled this out, and shot him. Man, was he surprised. I told Mallozi, and we agreed we shouldn't leave the body lying around, so he took care of it. At least I thought he did."

I edged toward the recliner.

Deloris steadied her gun on me .Don't move."

I froze mid-stride.

She shuffled over to the scooter. Once mounted, she pulled a sweater from her bed and wrapped it around the Glock. Then yanked the plug from the outlet. "You walk ahead of me. I don't want a mess in my room."

A mess?

Trembling, I looked toward the door. Could I get out in time?

As if reading my thoughts, she said. "Don't try to run. I'm a good shot. If I miss you, I might accidentally hit one of those old people. Wouldn't matter, they don't have long to live anyway. But I know you'd feel terrible about it, wouldn't you?"

"Uh-huh." I obediently held my hands up and walked out of the room.

Deloris shouted. "Are you nuts? Put your hands down. Do you want everyone to know what's going on? I'll have to start shooting."

I dropped my hands to my sides and lumbered to the exit. A dozen residents milled about in the lobby. I prayed none of them would approach us. I punched the button to open the door for Deloris. She indicated I should walk ahead.

"Where are we going?"

"None of your business. Just head to the pharmacy."

I started down the sidewalk, praying no one would be hurt because of me. By the time I got to the corner, the sound of the mobility scooter had stopped. . I veered around and cast a glance behind me. Deloris's transportation had stalled a few feet back. Her attention was on pushing buttons and jiggling levers.

"What's the problem, Deloris?"

"Darn thing died. Won't start. Stay right there." She used the butt of the gun to pound on the starter.

I put my hands on my hips. "The battery's dead. Don't you remember? You already went all the way to the police station and back? It wasn't plugged in long enough to recharge."

"No!" She pounded harder.

Recognizing my chance, I sneaked close, sprang onto the woman, and wrenched the gun from her hand.

"Wha..." She let go of the gun without much of a struggle. Then I was in control with the gun pointed at Deloris.

I thought to grab my phone, but realized my handbag, along with my cell phone, was in my car parked at the station. No one was around to hear my cries for help. Should I leave Deloris where she sat while I ran inside to get help? She probably couldn't shuffle far, if I hurried.

My problem was solved when I heard a one-sided conversation behind me. A woman, completely unaware of her surroundings, walked toward us engrossed in a phone call.

As soon as she got close enough to interrupt her conversation, I planned to ask her to call the police.

Deloris was a quick thinker. She raised her hands in the air and yelled. "Help! I'm being robbed."

The woman yanked the phone away from her ear and stared at me. "How awful. You're robbing an old lady who can't even walk."

Oh, for gosh sakes.

"No, I'm not. She was going to shoot me, and I took the gun away from her."

The woman turned and ran down the sidewalk, screaming. "Help. Police. Call the police. Robbery."

Why do these things always happen to me?

I slumped against the building to wait for the sirens.

Chapter Twenty-Nine

Deloris gripped the scooter handlebars and attempted to dismount. "Give me my gun."

"No. Sit down. You know you can't walk fast enough to get it from me. We'll wait for the police."

She settled back on the scooter and raised her hands again. I stared at Deloris. "Put your hands down. Nobody's going to believe I tried to rob you."

She smiled. "Yes they will. You're holding the gun."

Darn it. She had a point.

I dropped the Glock and kicked it into the grass.

Within a few minutes, a squad car pulled into the parking lot next to the sidewalk. Officer Farlow stepped from the driver's side and walked toward me with his gun drawn.

Crap.

I put my hands in the air and hyperventilated.

Deloris pointed at me and said, "She pulled a gun and tried to rob me."

I glanced her way. "I did not."

"Halloren, you've gone too far this time. Put your hands on your head."

"Okay." I laced my fingers on top of my head. Farlow holstered his weapon and proceeded to search me. I'd always been ticklish and stifled a giggle. It was not the time.

To Deloris, Officer Farlow said, "What happened, ma'am?"

Directing her innocent gaze at him, Deloris sniffed. "She was going to shoot me. I thought I was going to die."

The man straightened his shoulders and pulled his gun again. "Don't worry, ma'am. You're safe now."

I looked at his gun. "Can I put my hands down?"

"No."

"My shoulders ache."

"Just stay where you are and don't move. The lady said there was a weapon. Where is it?"

"It's in the grass at the side of the walk."

Farlow kept his pistol aimed at me while he scanned the area. "Where?"

"Over there." I jerked my head and pointed with my chin until he got the idea and located the gun.

"Now, can I put my hands down?"

"No."

Deloris managed to sound like a frightened little girl. "Don't let her go. She'll kill me."

"I've got her, ma'am. You're safe. I'm just waiting for backup, and we'll take her to jail."

Footsteps sounded behind me, and I was afraid to look. It sounded like the whole force had arrived.

A look of relief spread across Farlow's face. "Chief, I'm glad to see you."

Police Chief Melvin Stoddard studied me and Deloris, then turned his attention to Farlow. "What's the story, Officer?"

I looked on, hands on head, while Farlow related what he knew of the incident, which wasn't much.

Deloris said, "She tried to rob me."

"I did not."

The Chief and Farlow hovered over Deloris. "Are you alright now, ma'am?"

"I'm okay. I just want to go home, but my scooter died."

"Do you live at Beaver Creek? We'll have someone help you get back."

"Oh, thank you, Officer. I'm so grateful you arrived when you did."

I tried to be patient while they chatted, but finally raised my voice. "My shoulders are killing me. May I please put my hands down?"

Farlow looked at Stoddard. The chief nodded.

Officer Farlow leveled his gaze at me. "Alright, put 'em down. But stay where you are, and don't try anything."

Taking my hands from my head, I massaged my neck.

A deep voice came from behind me. "What happened here, Lauren?"

It was a voice I knew, and I wanted to cry. I pivoted to gaze into chocolate-brown eyes. "Jack Spencer. Thank goodness you're here. It's such a mess. Deloris D'agostino was taking me to the drugstore to kill me. Not really to the drugstore—to the alley beside the drugstore."

I stopped and searched his gaze. He wasn't getting

179

it.

I forged ahead. "We only got this far when her battery died. She got busy trying to get the scooter started again, and I got the gun away from her."

Jack tipped his head to the side and squinted at me.

I took a breath and continued. "Well, then some woman started screaming that I was robbing an old lady. And she ran away and called the police."

I paused for another breath. The story sounded like gibberish, even to me.

I had no choice but to finish. "Then officer Farlow came and Deloris told him I wanted to kill her. It's not even my gun. It's hers."

Jack closed his eyes for a moment, then opened them and gave me a reassuring smile. "We'll get it all sorted out down at the station."

He looked over my head at the chief. "Chief Stoddard, I'll drive Ms. Halloren to the station. You and Officer Farlow can get a statement from Mrs. D'agostino."

I stood on tiptoes to whisper in Jack's ear. "Deloris killed Camden Greene, the guy Clair and I found in the ravine."

Jack turned to the chief. "Since the scooter isn't working, maybe you can get Mrs. D'agostino a wheelchair. Then you should talk to her at the station."

Chief Stoddard turned away from Deloris. "Great idea, Agent Spencer. You take charge of Ms. Halloren while we take care of the victim."

Victim?

Officer Farlow jerked his head up and sputtered. "You better put handcuffs on the Halloren woman."

Jack put a hand up. "I can handle her."

Farlow began to sputter again, but Stoddard laid a hand on his shoulder. "Just do what Agent Spencer said."

Farlow's face flushed and his eyes grew wide. "Former agent. He's a civilian."

Melvin studied Farlow, then said, "Go get the wheelchair."

The officer shut his mouth, pivoted, and stormed toward the nursing home entrance.

Jack and I left Chief Stoddard to comfort Deloris and walked to Jack's sedan. I imagined we were on a date when he opened the door for me. It was a short drive to the station, but I wished it would last forever. I sat speechless during the drive, while I admired the profile of the man who had saved me.

Jack shifted the car into park at the station, and I found words. "I'm so glad you showed up when you did. What would I have done without you? I'd be in handcuffs in Farlow's squad car."

He turned to me with a smile that raised the temperature inside the car. "Glad I could help."

I sucked in a breath before I could speak. "How did you happen to be there?

Jack leaned back against the seat. "Heard it on the police radio and caught up with Chief Stoddard. I had a feeling I needed to be there."

He chuckled while he unbuckled his seatbelt. "I don't usually carry the radio, but thought it best while in Evelynton. Not much goes on in this burg, but you seem to show up in police business quite a lot."

Chapter Thirty

My body was about to melt into the seat. I wanted to stay in the quiet security of Jack's presence, forever. Would have loved to pull my feet up onto the seat and lay my head on his shoulder. I released my seatbelt and might have done just that, had I not regained my sanity. Instead, I opened the car door, and with as much composure as possible, I followed him into the police station.

Once inside, Jack guided me to a chair, in which I obediently sat. He continued to the chief's office. I didn't see Deloris D'agostino anywhere. Maybe she was in a cell. Maybe they'd bring her in another entrance. Either way, I would be happy not to see her again, ever. I closed my eyes and thought of better things.

The clock showed it had been about thirty minutes when I opened my eyes to Officer Farlow's voice. "Ms. Halloren, would you step over to my desk? I'll take your statement. Shouldn't take long, and you'll be able to go home."

Once again Farlow was polite as he took my statement.

Melvin Stoddard came to the desk. "The gun we found at the scene is registered to Mrs. D'agostino. She has confessed to threatening you with it and won't be pressing charges."

"That's a relief. Thanks for letting me know."

Stoddard smiled and shook his head. "We're also looking into some other statements she's made. The woman hasn't shut up since we brought her in. Please accept my apologies for the inconvenience."

Stoddard directed a stare at Farlow until the younger officer stood up and added, "I'm very sorry for the mix up."

After I'd signed the statement, I scanned the waiting area. Jack was nowhere in sight. So with a sigh, I walked out of the police station, alone. My car sat parked where I'd left it. Maybe I should walk. Did I even have the energy to drive?

"Would you like a ride?" Jack leaned against his tan sedan parked next to mine. My hero.

"Oh, yes please. I'm not sure I could find my way home. I thought you'd gone already."

"Without saying goodbye? Not a chance. I needed to let the Evelynton Police Department do their job."

"Let me get my handbag from the car." With a new burst of energy, I climbed into the Chrysler and grabbed my bag.

When I returned, Jack opened his passenger door for me, and I slid in.

Snuggled into the seat, I realized my energy had left me once again. All I could say was, "Thank you for waiting for me." After that, we rode in silence.

Before I knew it, we were parked in my driveway. I prepared to leave the little sanctuary.

It had been years since I'd dated—not that this was a date—so I wrestled with how to leave the car. Would Jack get out and open my door for me? Or should I get out myself?

Question answered. He reached over to take my hand before it reached the door handle. Then he leaned over and kissed me. The romantic thing would have been to close my eyes, but I was so surprised, I stared at him.

My hero leaned back. "Are you alright now?"

"Oh, I'm wonderful. Just glad it's over. The ordeal with Deloris, not the kiss. I'm not glad that's over. In fact, let me try it again." I moved toward him, stopped abruptly and undid my seatbelt, then leaned into Jack for a kiss. This time with my eyes closed. Much better. We lingered close before pulling away at the perfect time.

I couldn't stop staring into his eyes and hoped I didn't look much like a love-sick teenager. "Thank you, for everything. Don't know what I'd have done without you."

"Glad I could be of service. Good thing I happened to be in town. Unfortunately, now I have to get back to the city. My business and all." A light smile lit his lips "But I'll be in touch."

He opened his car door and got out. Still perplexed as to current protocol, I slipped out of my side on my own.

We climbed the concrete steps of the Cape Cod and he waited while I unlocked the door.

Then Jack winked at me, strode back to his car, and drove away.

I pulled the heavy oak door closed, glided into the living room, and slumped onto the sofa, too tired to walk any farther.

Mason launched himself from the floor and landed gently on my lap. "Mason, let's watch old movies. I can't deal with reality this evening."

I flipped channels until Susan Hayward appeared on the screen. Slipping out of my shoes, I stretched out on the sofa. Mason fell asleep on my stomach.

Thirty minutes later the phone in my handbag began to ring. Mason lifted his head and uttered a groan. I glanced at my bag on the floor and stroked the cat's silky head. "Not now. I don't want to talk about it, not to anyone." Mason and I waited for the ringing to stop, then settled in to watch the rest of the movie.

Chapter Thirty-One

O pening my eyes to beams of sunlight dancing on my bedroom walls, I realized I'd had a full night's sleep for the first time in weeks. In no hurry to get on with my day, I took my coffee to lounge on the back porch. It was perfect. The sun warmed me. A soft breeze swayed the trees. A chorus of bird songs were clearer and more melodious than usual.

Mason's cat entrance in the screen door popped open and his furry head appeared. With a faint meow, he curled up at my feet.

"Mason, this is the life. Wish I could stay in my pajamas all day."

The feline rolled onto his back and performed a long, slow stretch.

"Look at you. Free to do as you please. Sleep, play, and eat. Sleep, play, and eat."

My morning relaxation slipped away, as a to-do list forced its way into my brain. I ticked off the necessary chores of my existence. "But I have to work. Some research for that Spring article. And I should visit

Louise. She and the other residents are probably upset at the business with Deloris."

Mason sat up and put his front paws on my knee, allowing me to scratch behind his ears. "I better go. You enjoy the morning, you free spirit."

I downed the last of my coffee and left my little backyard utopia.

~

I drove across town thinking of advice Rarity had given me. "You create the climate of your day by the energy you give it." Rolling down the driver-side window, I breathed in the fresh morning air. At the first stop sign, I slid across the seat and rolled down the passenger window. The breeze flowed in one window and out the other, taking all my worries with it, as I drove across town. It was wonderful. I felt like a ten-year-old, without a care in the world.

A prime parking spot opened across from Beaver Creek and I laughed as I whipped the car into it. A gift from my new attitude. Then I caught a glimpse of my refection in the rear-view mirror. Not the lovely free spirit look I'd been going for. More like an escaped spirit. Escaped from a lunatic asylum.

After spending five minutes pulling tangles from my hair, I marched across the street to the nursing home.

Pushing through the doors, I stopped short. Words rang out, loud and clear. "Lauren Halloren, my hero!"

Helen, Beaver Creek activities director, strode toward me, waving a newspaper. "Your story about the residents appeared this morning on page three. It was perfect. The phone hasn't stopped ringing since I got in at nine o'clock. Everyone wants to sign up to visit a resident. The whole town is on board."

"No kidding? I'm glad people were moved by the piece." I'd never experienced such enthusiastic reactions to my writing. More of a "Ho hum. Wasn't that nice. What's on the next page?" sort of thing.

Helen put her arm around my shoulder. "If this keeps up, all the needy residents will have Extended Family and I'll start doubling up. The article was wonderful. You were a god-send. Thank you so much."

"Don't thank me. All I did was write the truth. Evelynton is full of good people who only needed to be made aware of the situation."

"It's so much more than that. You opened the heart of Evelynton and called people to action. Thinking about the good you've done brings tears to my eyes." She began reading sections of my article to me.

I remembered the passages and had to admit they sounded pretty good when read aloud.

I can only handle so much praise, and searched for a way out of the spotlight.

Helen paused in her oration, and I jumped in. "Love to stay and talk, but I'm on my way to check on Louise. Worried about her since her neighbor was arrested. It must be confusing for her." I slid my foot to the side and edged around Helen. "So glad the article had an impact." I turned and jogged toward Louise's room.

I'd made it half way when Helen called after me. "Lauren, wait. Almost forgot." I hit the brakes and swiveled toward her, ready to continue my retreat if she started reading to me again. "The article about the D'agostino's arrest was on the front page of the paper.

You're not only our hero, you're a hero to the whole town."

"You know me. I wasn't heroic. All I did was stumble into the wrong place—twice."

"Lauren, I know you don't like publicity, but you should play this up. Many callers asked if you'd autograph their newspaper articles when they came in. You should write a book about how you exposed a theft ring and captured a murderer. It would put Evelynton on the map. Maybe you should be grand marshal of the Founder's day parade."

No.

Dumbfounded, I didn't have words for a reply and simply stared at Helen.

"Anyway, I told the callers to bring the newspaper along, in case they caught you here. Alternately, we could have a signing here at Beaver Creek."

I could almost see the lightbulb go on above Helen's head. "That's it. A book-signing, um newspaper signing. We'll set up a table for you in Evelyn's Party Room and serve refreshments."

"Oh. Let's not do that. All the excitement will die down in a day or two. They'll forget about me."

"Think about it. The citizens I talked to were determined. If they don't find you here, they might show up on your doorstep. Do you know how easy it is to find someone's address in Evelynton?"

"They wouldn't go to that much trouble for an autograph, would they?"

Helen nodded.

I had visions of autograph hunters knocking on my door at all hours of the day. "Now that I think about it, set up a time and let everyone know I'll be here on a certain date—for one hour."

"Oh no, at least two hours. And plan on extending it if the need arises. You wouldn't want to miss anyone. Trust me, as activities director, I know how these things go."

"Okay, two, but that's all." Not waiting for another argument, I turned and fled.

I found Louise sitting in her oversized recliner, feel dangling a few inches above the floor. "How are you, Louise?"

She aimed the remote control at the television and clicked it off. "Lauren dear, come in. I'm just dandy. And how's your day?"

"Not as peaceful as I'd expected. I came to see about you."

I crouched down beside her chair. "Have you been lonely this morning since Deloris moved out?" I hesitated to say Deloris was arrested. How much did the elderly remember or understand?

Louise grinned. "Lonely? Not a chance. More company now than ever. You'd think I was some kind of celebrity. People stop by and want to know all about what it was like to live across from a murderer. Did I suspect? Did she tell me about her secret life?"

Louise's laugh tinkled like tiny bells. "I'm thinking of charging a fee to tell the story. Start up a little business of my own."

I moved to sit on the edge of Louise's bed. "That's a relief. I thought you might have been upset. The other residents weren't distressed over the whole thing? Did anyone indicate they were afraid to stay here?"

Laughing full out, Louise slapped the side of her chair. "Of course not. We haven't had this much excitement in the last decade. More fun than watching Perry Mason reruns."

Chapter Thirty-Two

I shoved the Chrysler into park, opened the car door, and had one foot on the ground before noticing the scene unfolding on my neighbor's doorstep. I had to force my mouth to close. Murine Baron was enfolded in a passionate embrace with a man! Towering over her, the stranger stepped back to gaze into her eyes. His broad hands engulfed her thin shoulders. Then she stood on tiptoe to kiss him again.

What was this? Murine, with a boyfriend? I pulled my foot back into the car and waited. Should I stay in the Chrysler? Should I walk into the house and pretend not to notice?"

When the man turned, and I saw him in profile, I gripped the steering wheel to keep from falling out of the car. Clive Baron, Murine's missing husband.

He was alive. Even after the body in the woods had been identified, in the back of my mind I'd thought Murine had shot her husband with his 12-guage.

At least this man looked like Clive. There was still the possibility of alien abduction.

I waited but the hot sun was making the inside of

the car unbearable. Couldn't sit there all day. I climbed out and slammed the door, hoping to give the impression I'd just arrived.

Murine twirled to face me. She wore a big smile. "Lauren, look who's home."

I feigned surprise. "Hello, you two. Clive, I see you're back from your fishing trip. Did you have good luck?"

I didn't expect an answer. He hadn't spoken to me in over a year since I'd been his neighbor. But with his arm still around Murine, he actually smiled. "I had very good luck. Not so much with the fish, but I learned what was important in life."

His voice was deep and rough, but not as gruff as I'd imagined it to be.

"After Murine gave me the ultimatum, it took a while to understand what I'd be losing. I know I have to treat her better. She deserves a loving husband. This woman is the most important thing in my life, and I should handle her like a precious gift. Like a priceless pearl, a treasure of great worth."

My mouth might have been hanging open. Not only had Clive spoken, but he was poetic—even biblical.

Murine gazed up at her husband. "I didn't tell her about the ultimatum, honey. I keep our private affairs to myself. I just waited for you to come to your senses. And you did."

Clive let out a loud laugh. "I should have known. You are a good woman. You've always thought of me first. But, I don't mind if the whole town knows."

He peered over at me. "She told me to get out until I could become a real husband. Kicked me out of the house. This woman doesn't get mad often, but when she does, she means business."

Murine's cheeks turned pink, and she gazed up at him. "I'm sorry it had to come to that, Clive."

Clive lowered his voice and stared deep into his wife's eyes. "It was worth it. I was a prideful, unkind man and thought only of myself. I want all my friends to know, so they won't make the same mistake."

Murine beamed and the two of them went into their house, hand in hand.

I stood in the drive for a minute before continuing up the steps to my door. I'd like to experience a love like that. *Someday.*

Thirty-Three

Warm rays of the late afternoon sun filled the back porch. I opened a bottle of wine and carried it along with three glasses from the kitchen. After handing Clair and Anita their glasses I set mine on the little wicker table. Anita lounged in one of the matching chairs with her legs stretched out in front of her. My friends were frequent visitors to my back porch during the summer months. What was unusual was the sight of Clair sitting on the floor. She trailed a twig across the floorboards for Mason to chase.

I watched her for a while, then couldn't resist. "Clair, I have to ask. Are those jeans you're wearing? Didn't know you owned any."

Anita laughed. "And did you notice she's wearing flats? Shocked me that she could walk in anything but high heels."

She looked at Clair. "Doesn't it throw you off balance?"

Clair pointed the twig at Anita. "No, I can walk

perfectly fine. This is my new casual attire. From now on, when I'm not working, I'll be the picture of comfort." She glanced at both of us. "And since we're on the subject of my changed lifestyle, I'm in the market for a house."

Anita sat up straight. "No kidding? I thought you loved your apartment. Great security. No weeds to pull or lawn to mow."

Pulling Mason onto her lap, Clair twisted to face Anita. "I'm tired of apartment living. I want a yard and maybe a porch like this. I could get a grill, and have cook-outs. So, since I'd be looking at houses and wandering around yards, I needed shoes that wouldn't sink in the dirt and jeans to fit in with the country life. I can't wait to get my hands dirty and plant flowers."

Anita looked at me. I shrugged. She returned her gaze to Clair. "Flowers and dirt? You might ruin your manicure."

Clair contemplated her perfectly smoothed and painted nails. "That's okay. I'll wear them short. Don't act so surprised. I told you I wanted a change of life." She held out her glass for me to pour the wine. "Only half-way, please."

I ventured a question. "Why now?"

Clair continued. "You know, girls, I know almost everyone in town, but I don't have a clue as to who they really are. Do you understand? I know them as they relate to my business, but not as real people. Lauren, I read your newspaper article about the elderly at Beaver Creek. It really touched me. I not only want to adopt a resident, I want to know my neighbors. Really know them, as friends."

"Huh." Anita reached into the potato chip bag and

pulled out a handfull.

"Anita, you have always had a house in the country. You know everyone in town and people love you."

Anita stuck a chip in her mouth. "It's just the way I am. I don't think everyone should live like I do."

Clair gestured with her glass. "And let me tell you, the next man I date will be someone who is down to earth. He's not going have to dress up all the time, and he's not going to be impressed by expensive clothes. He'll love taking long walks, and sitting by the fire on cold nights."

Anita grinned. "And will he ride a motorcycle?"

Clair was quick to answer. "Ugh. No." She paused and added, "At least, I doubt that will be one of his hobbies."

"He's going to be more like your Jake, Anita."

"My husband is a keeper, that's the truth. You wouldn't be wrong finding someone like him. It might take time, though. Jake and I've been married a long time. We had to get accustomed to one another. You'll have to be patient. Can't fall for the first one you meet."

"I can wait. I want a real relationship. Not just dating."

Mason purred as Clair rubbed his ears. "And as soon as I move and have a yard, I'm going to adopt a dog from the canine rescue. You said you liked Mason's veterinarian, Lauren. What's his name?"

"Michael Barry."

Anita cut her eyes to Clair. "Ha. I'm beginning to see the light. Dr. Barry is single and really cute."

Clair smiled. "He is nice looking. But the best

thing about him is he's down to earth. And friendly. I saw him at the grocery store. He showed me how to choose the best peaches. Isn't that sweet?"

"I think you'll be happy with your lifestyle change, Clair. Mine was sort of forced on me. I hated to leave the condo in Florida. But I have to admit, this house and small-town living is growing on me."

I set the wine bottle on the floor and picked up my glass. The wicker creaked as I sank into my chair. My eyes and thoughts drifted to the neighbors. In the last weeks, I'd seen Murine and Clive in town, together, holding hands. It had taken them a while— some hard truth, and an ultimatum—but they had found a great relationship.

A cell phone rang in the distance. Clair and Anita said, "Not mine" in unison.

"Darn. Left the phone in the house. I just got comfortable. They'll probably call back."

"Clair peered at me with an impish grin. Better get it. It might be the chance of a lifetime."

Anita laughed. "Maybe you won the Clearinghouse Giveaway. You could be set for life."

The phone continued to ring. I called to it. "Alright, I'm coming." I hauled myself out of my chair and into the kitchen, catching the phone before it went to voicemail.

"Lauren." The sound took my breath away.

I managed a weak, "Hello, Jack."

"I'll be in Evelynton this weekend. I was wondering if you'd be free for dinner?"

The End

Don't Miss Heart Strings, Book One.

Born and raised in northeastern Indiana, Lynne Waite Chapman is a lover of mystery and suspense. In September of 2016, she published her first cozy mystery. Her debut novel, Heart Strings—first in the Evelynton Murder series—was a 2016 semi-finalist in the American Christian Fiction Writers Association Genesis contest. Her second novel, Heart Beat, published in 2017, continues the series.

Lynne Waite Chapman began her writing career with fifteen years of composing weekly non-fiction content for the BellaOnline.com Hair site, drawing on her thirty plus years as a hairdresser. Retiring the Hair site, she has spent the last twelve years penning weekly content for the BellaOnline.com Christian Living site.

She is a regular contributor of devotions for several print publications, and has written articles for many church bulletins and newsletters. She has also contributed articles to numerous internet publications.

She currently resides in northern Indiana with one West Highland White Terrier

Made in the USA
Lexington, KY
19 January 2018